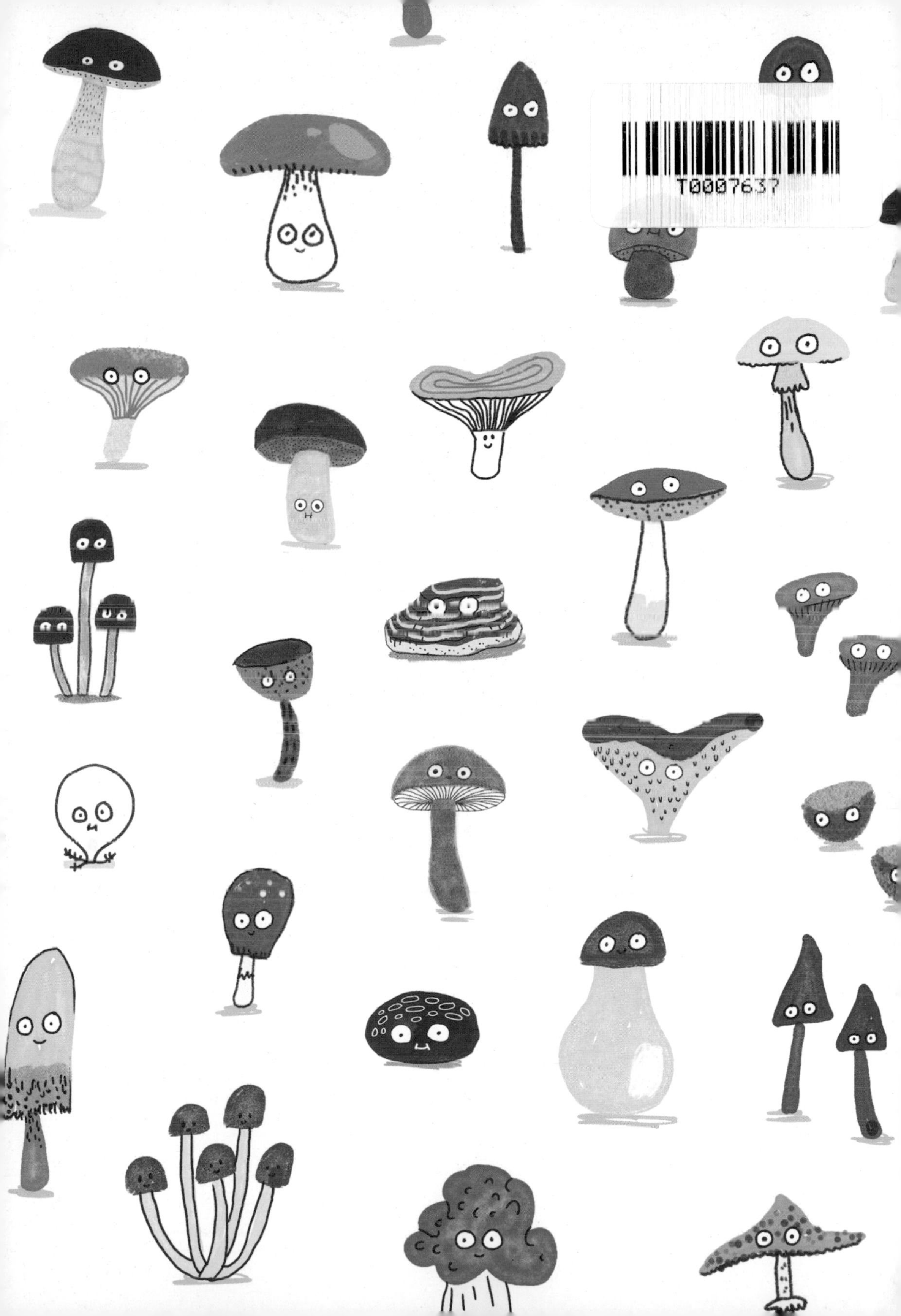

THE MUSHROOM FAN CLUB

ELISE GRAVEL

DRAWN & QUARTERLY

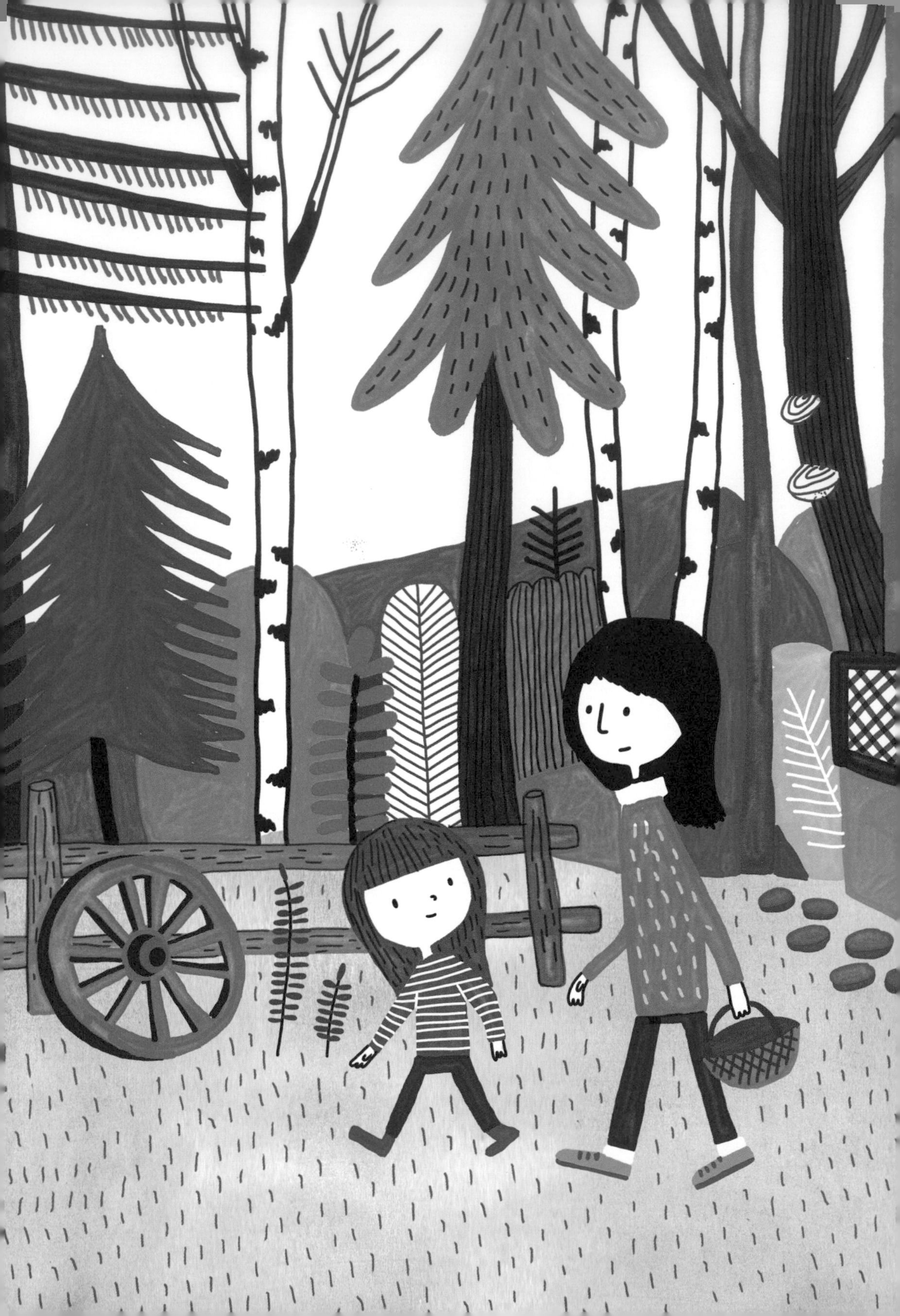

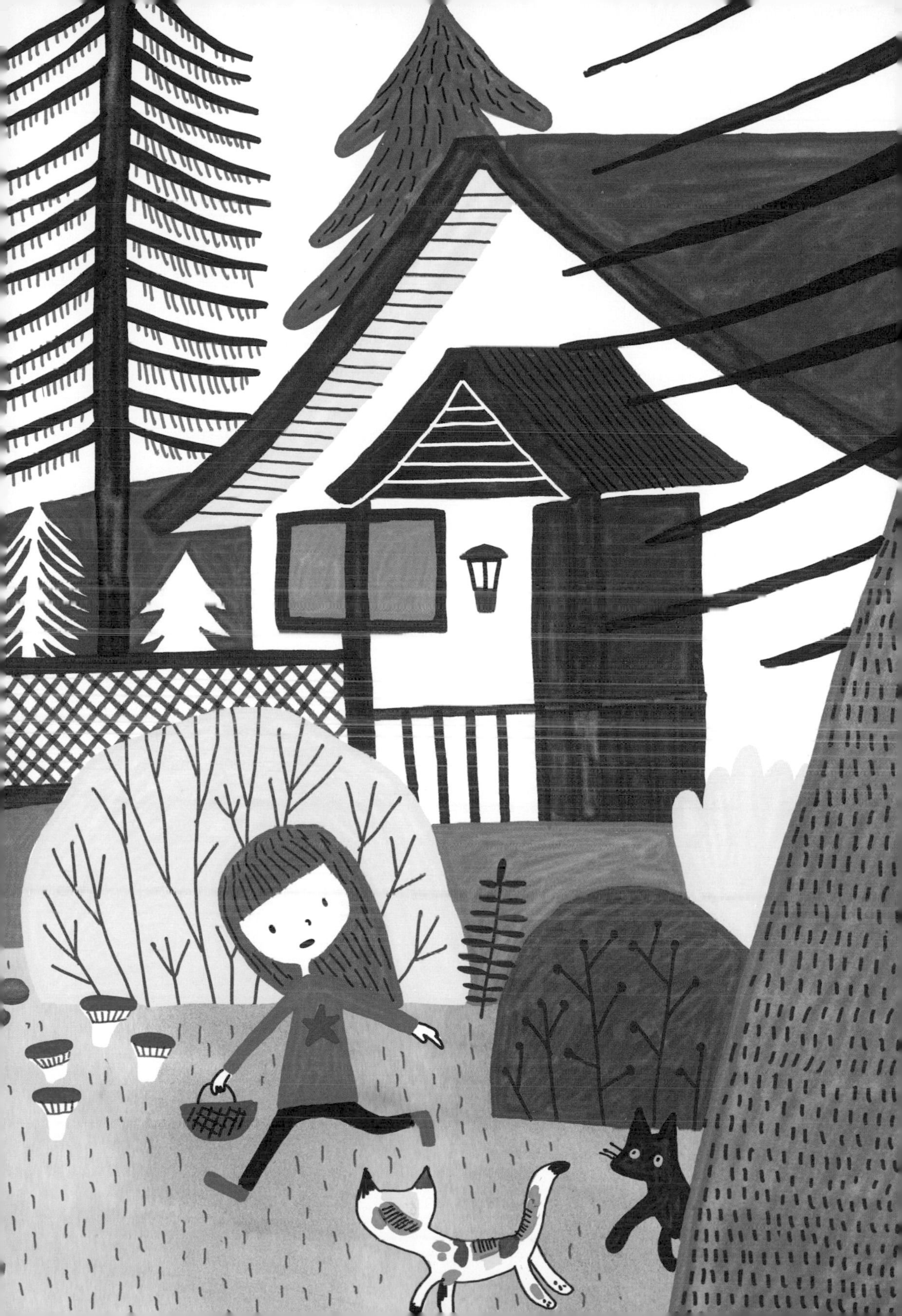

You know what I love? Walking in the woods and looking for mushrooms with my kids. It's like a treasure hunt that nature organized just for us!

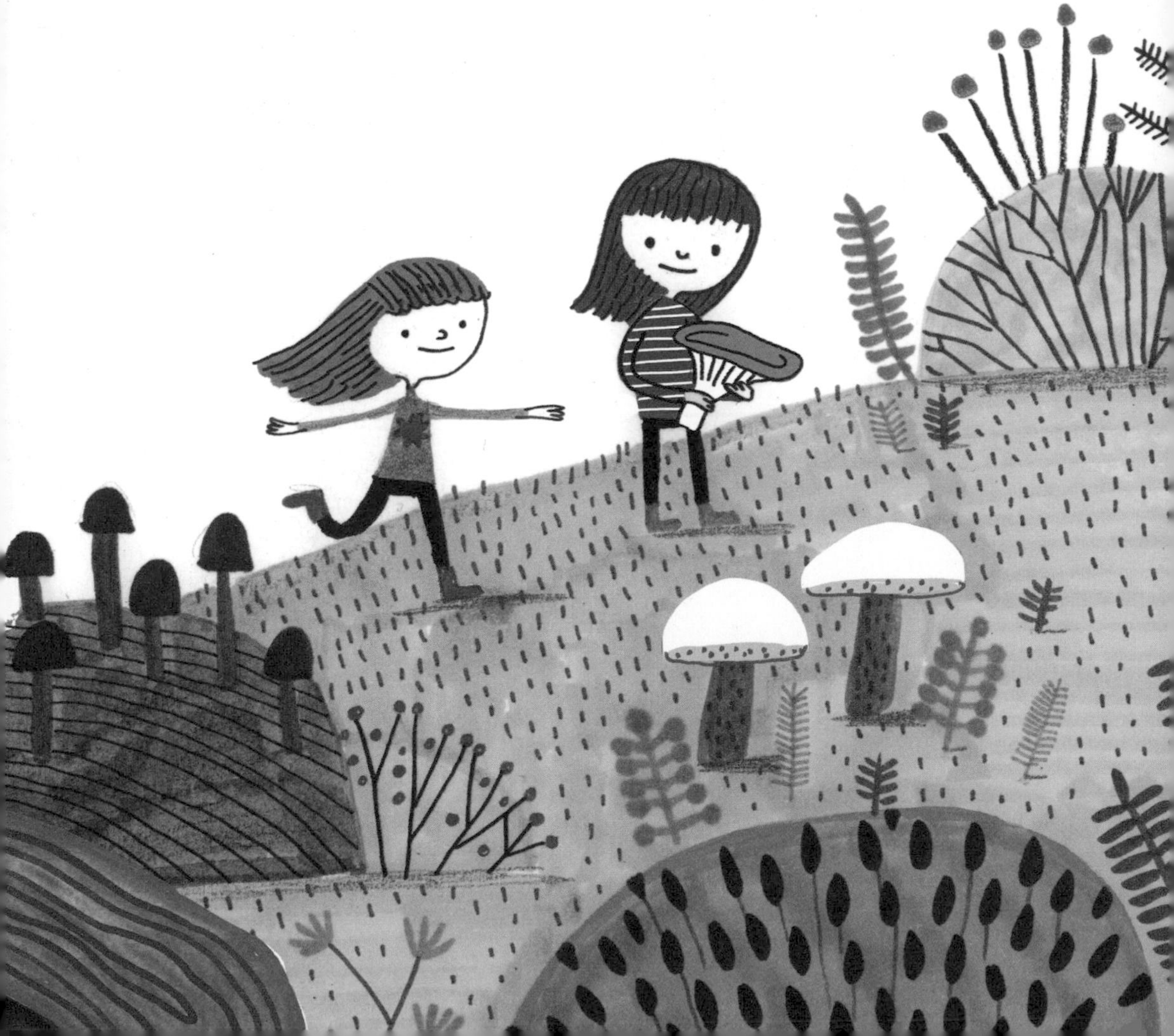

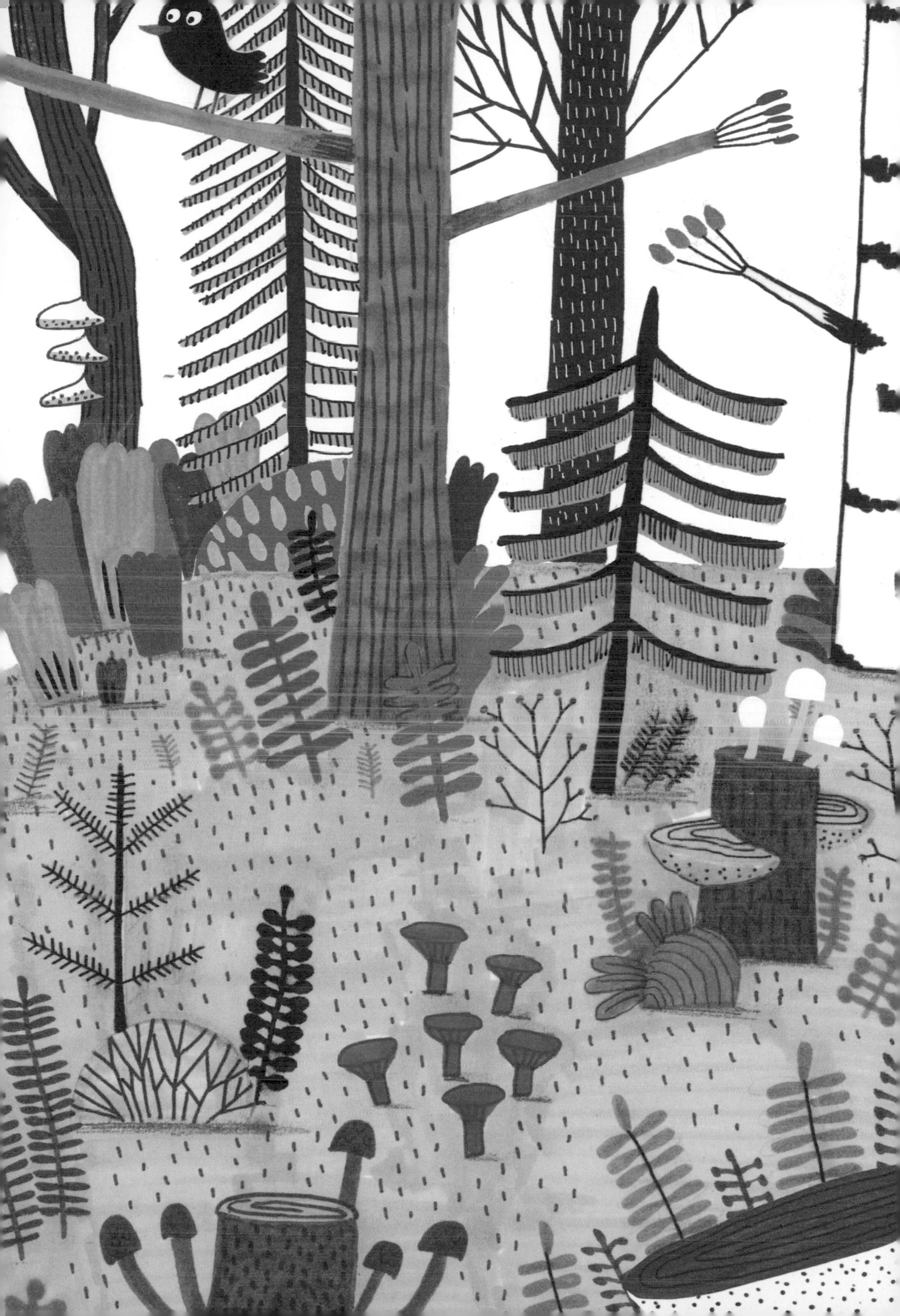

I'm obsessed with bizarre creatures,
and mushrooms are certainly strange!

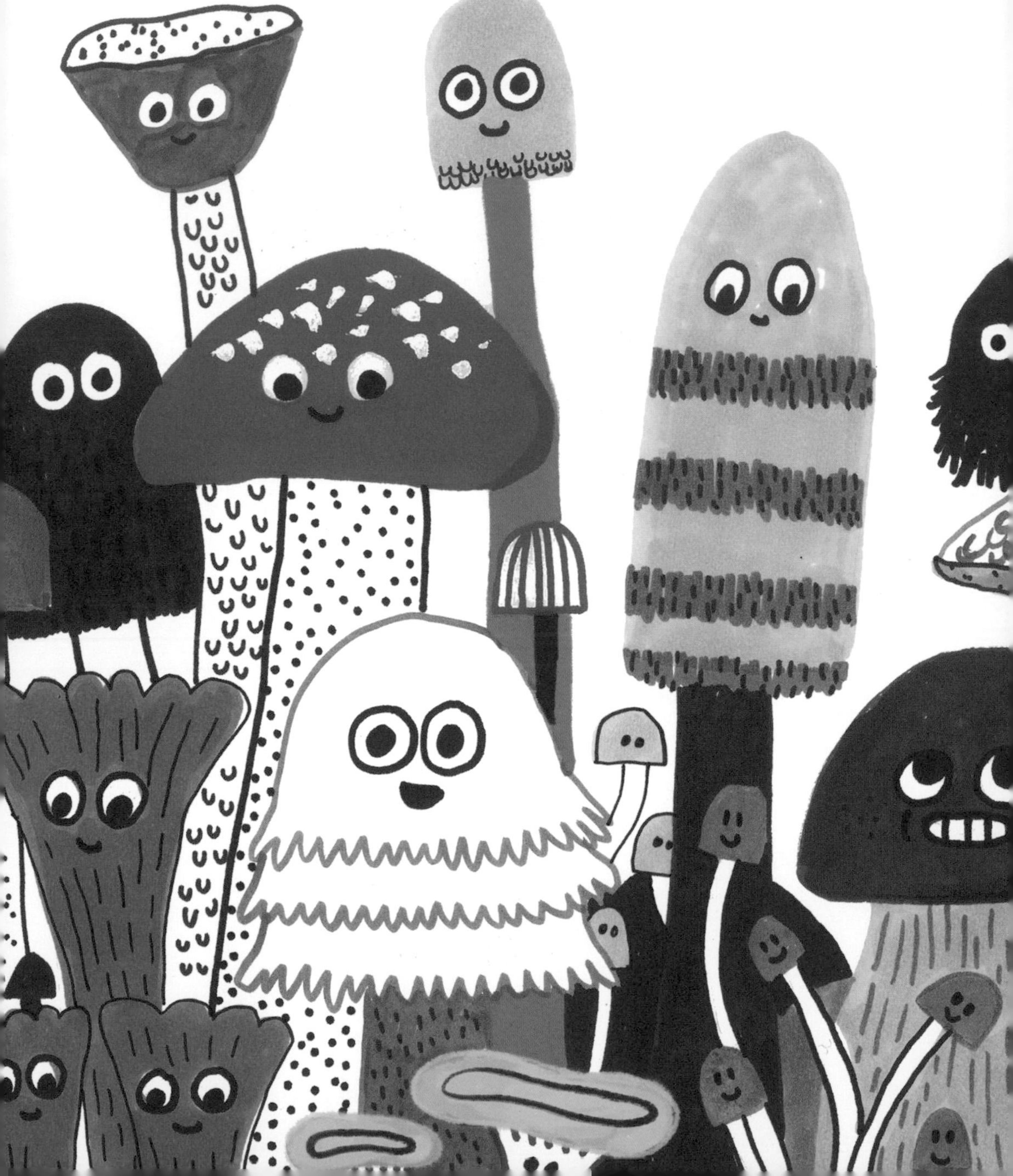

They look like aliens
from outer space.

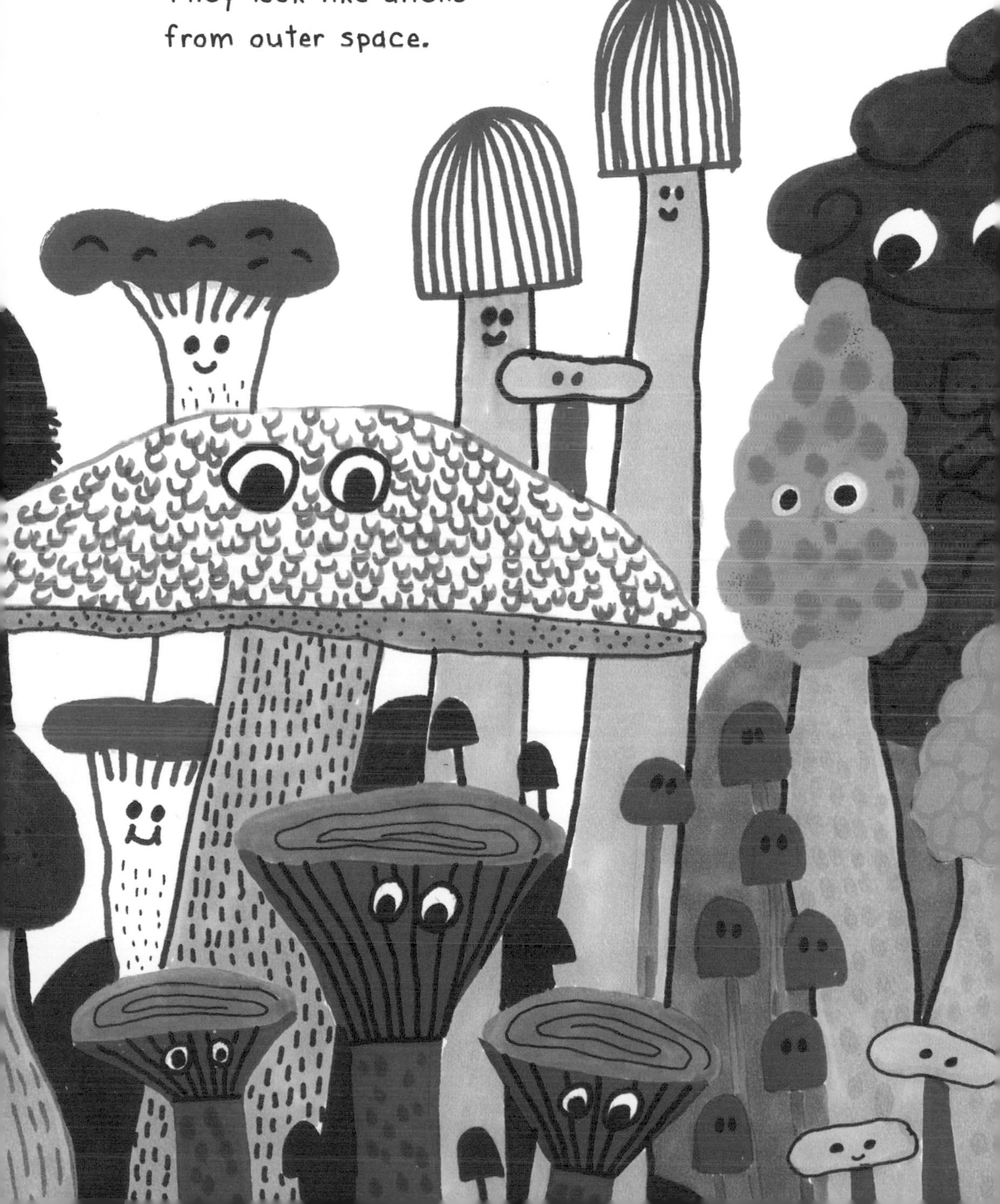

Mushrooms are not plants or animals. They are a kingdom of their own: the realm of FUNGI.

Many mushrooms look like the one I've drawn here, but not all of them. They come in many shapes, sizes, and colours!

Their smells differ wildly, too. Some stink horribly; others have a delicious perfume.

There are some next to my cottage that smell like maple syrup!

PARTS OF THE

MUSHROOM

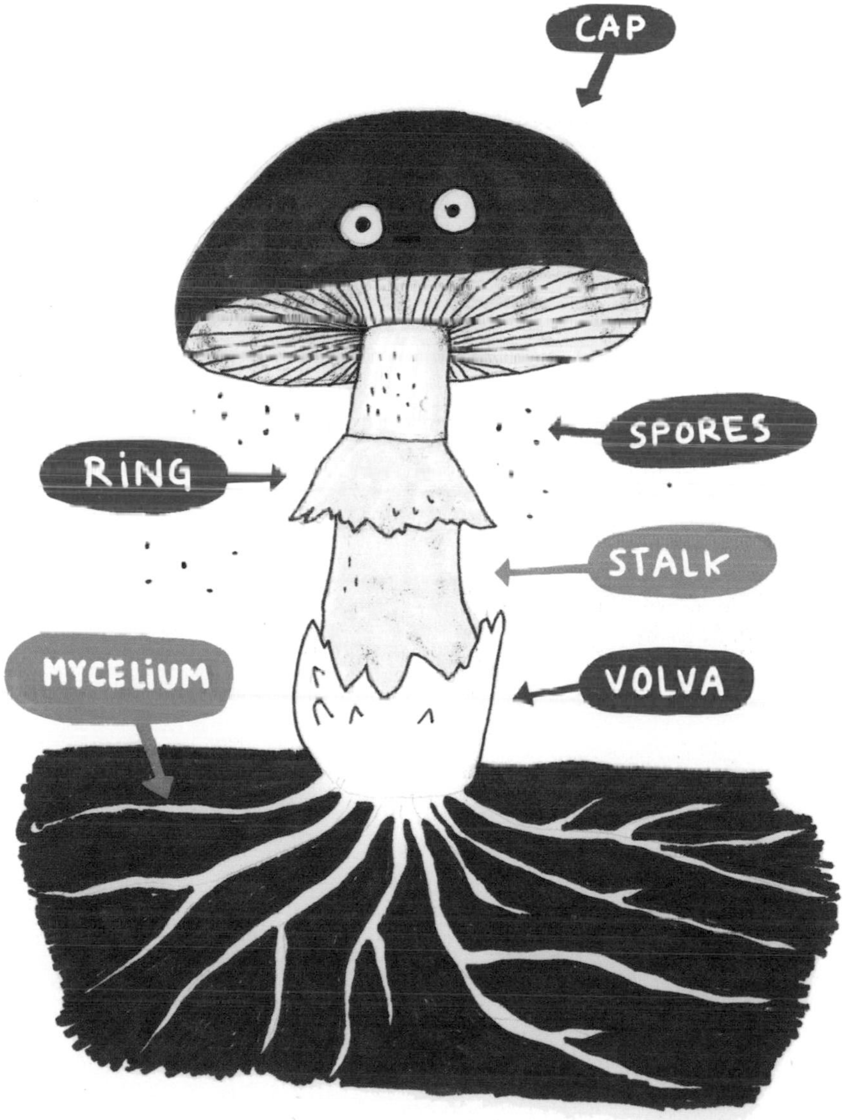
CAP
SPORES
RING
STALK
MYCELIUM
VOLVA

When you try to identify a mushroom, you have to look under its cap. You'll find clues under there!

Some have gills that are like paper-thin blades. There are thousands of different mushrooms like this, including the kinds found at grocery stores.

Others have little needles, and some have tiny holes, like a sponge.

It's through these various types of underbellies that they produce and release

which are a bit like seeds. This is how mushrooms reproduce.

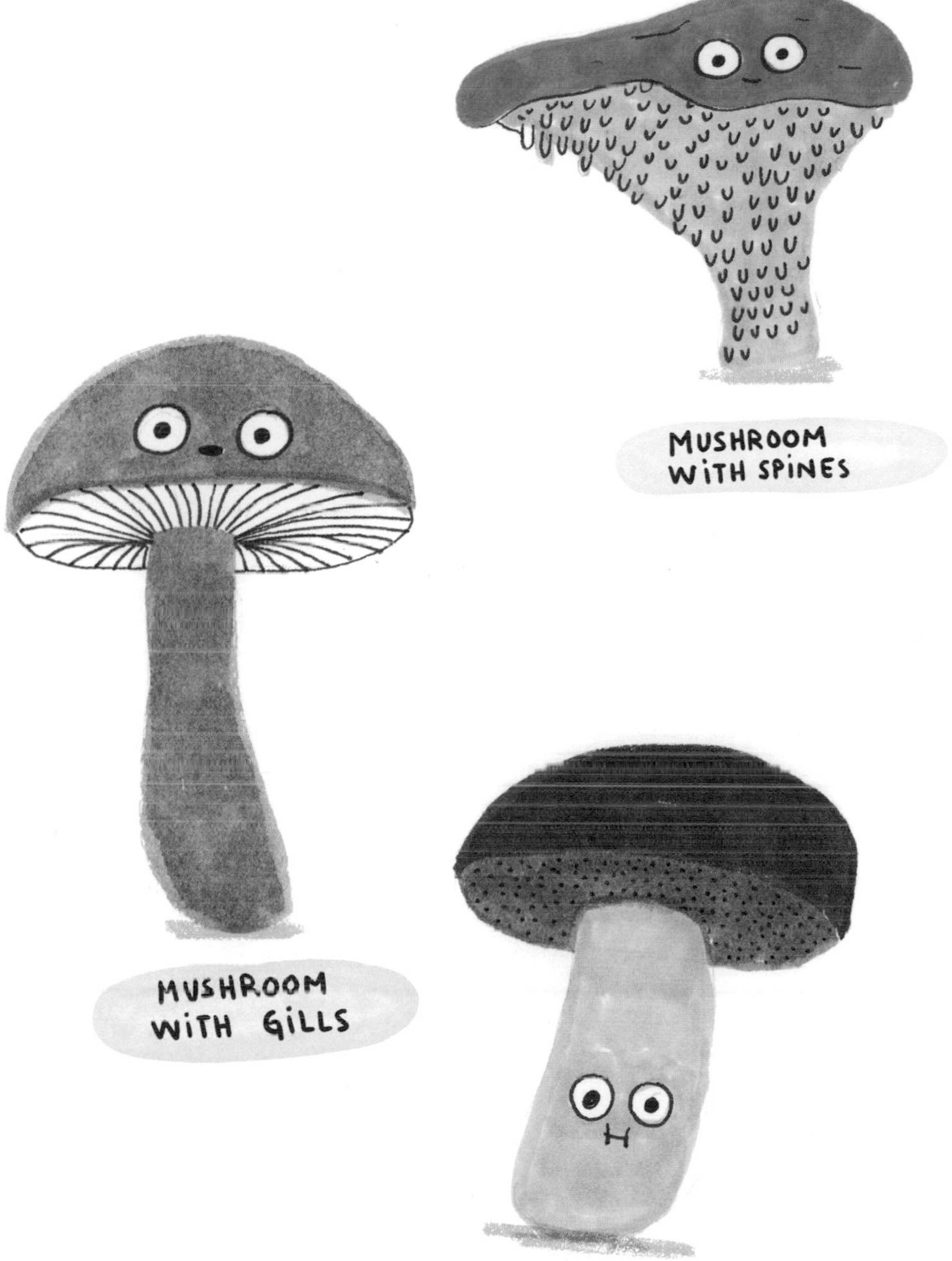
MUSHROOM WITH SPINES
MUSHROOM WITH GILLS
MUSHROOM WITH PORES

Some mushrooms grow in the grass, others in dead leaves or on rotten wood or even on living trees.

Some are so tiny we can't even see them, and others are as big as a baseball field!

I don't know them all. There are too many. There are

MILLIONS

of fungus species around the world.

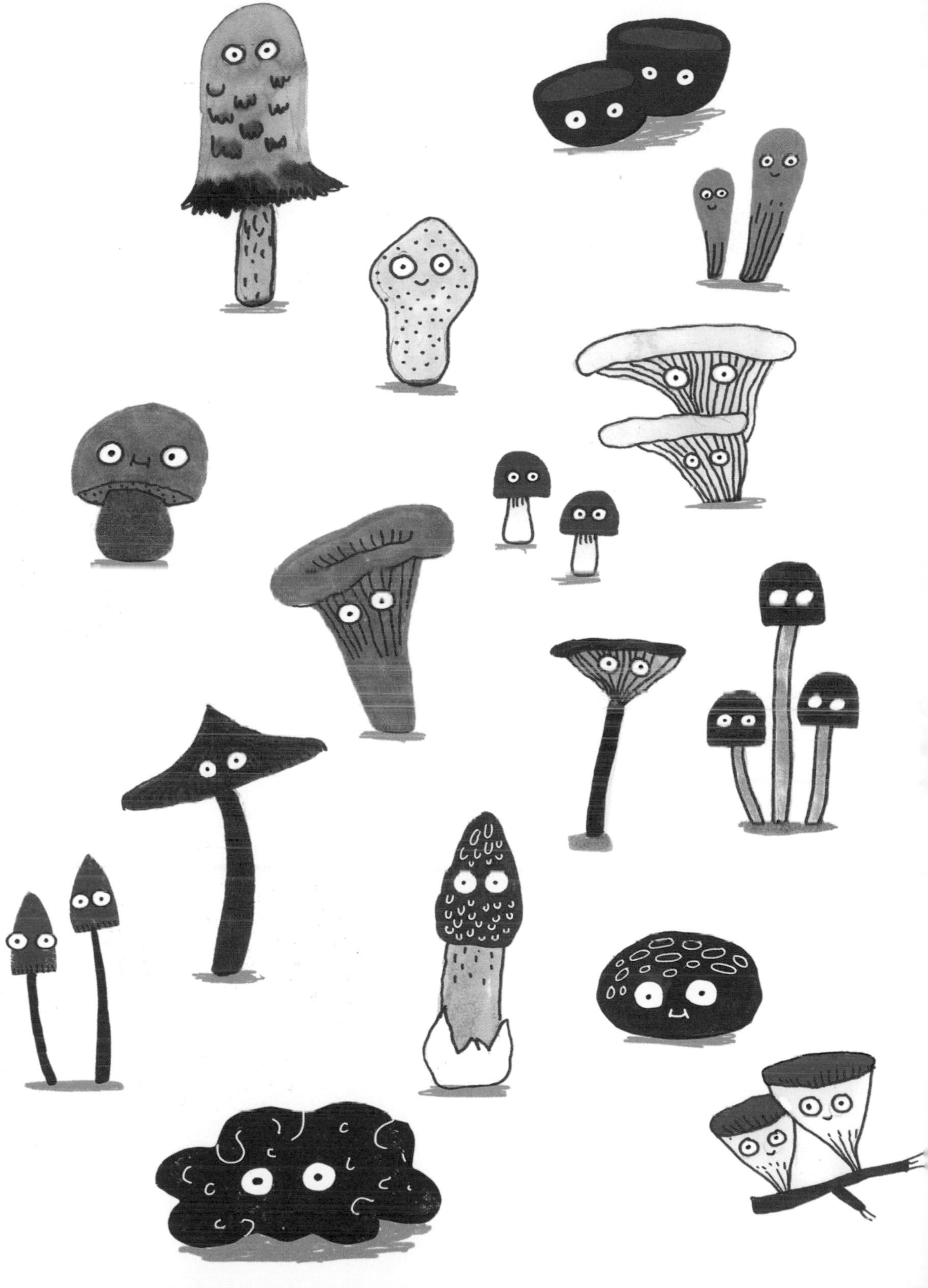

Some people know a lot more about mushrooms than I do. They are called

MYCOLOGISTS.

I am no expert: I'm an amateur. I just love looking at mushrooms.

The proof that I'm no expert?
I draw them with eyes!

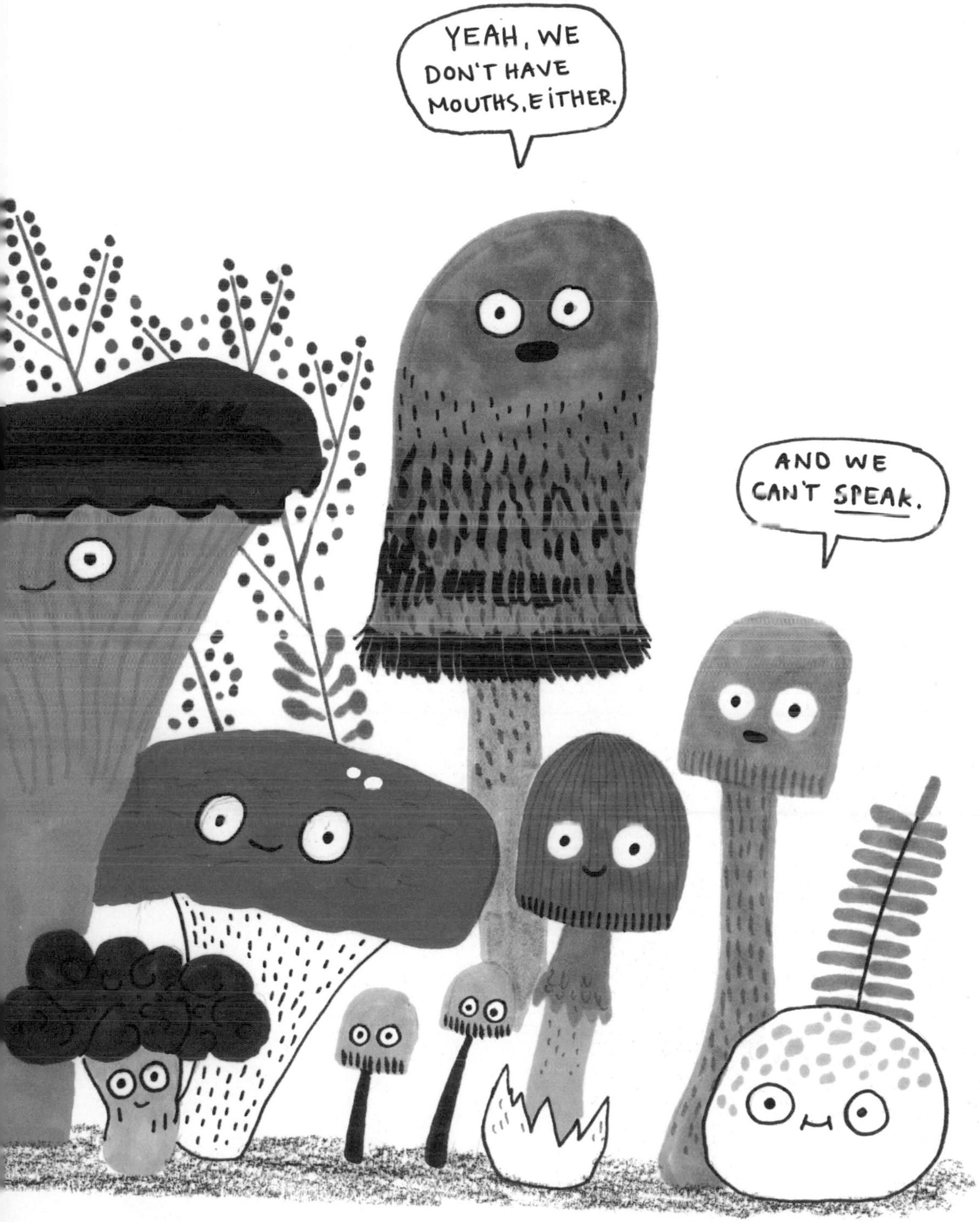
YEAH, WE DON'T HAVE MOUTHS, EITHER.
AND WE CAN'T SPEAK.

But I'm not the only one who likes finding mushrooms. Many animals and bugs like them, too! When you walk in the woods, you might encounter some of these wild mycologists.

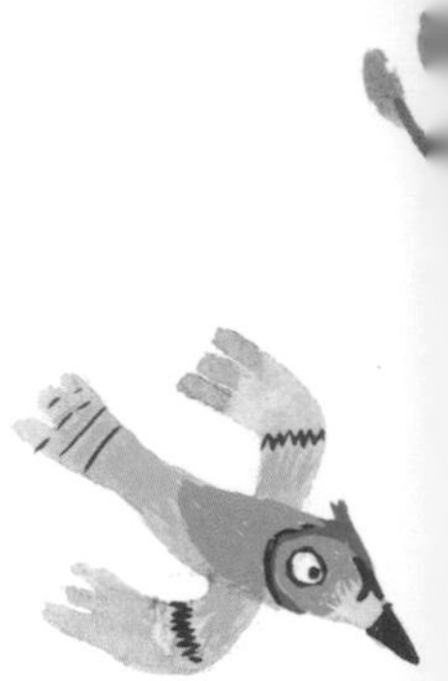

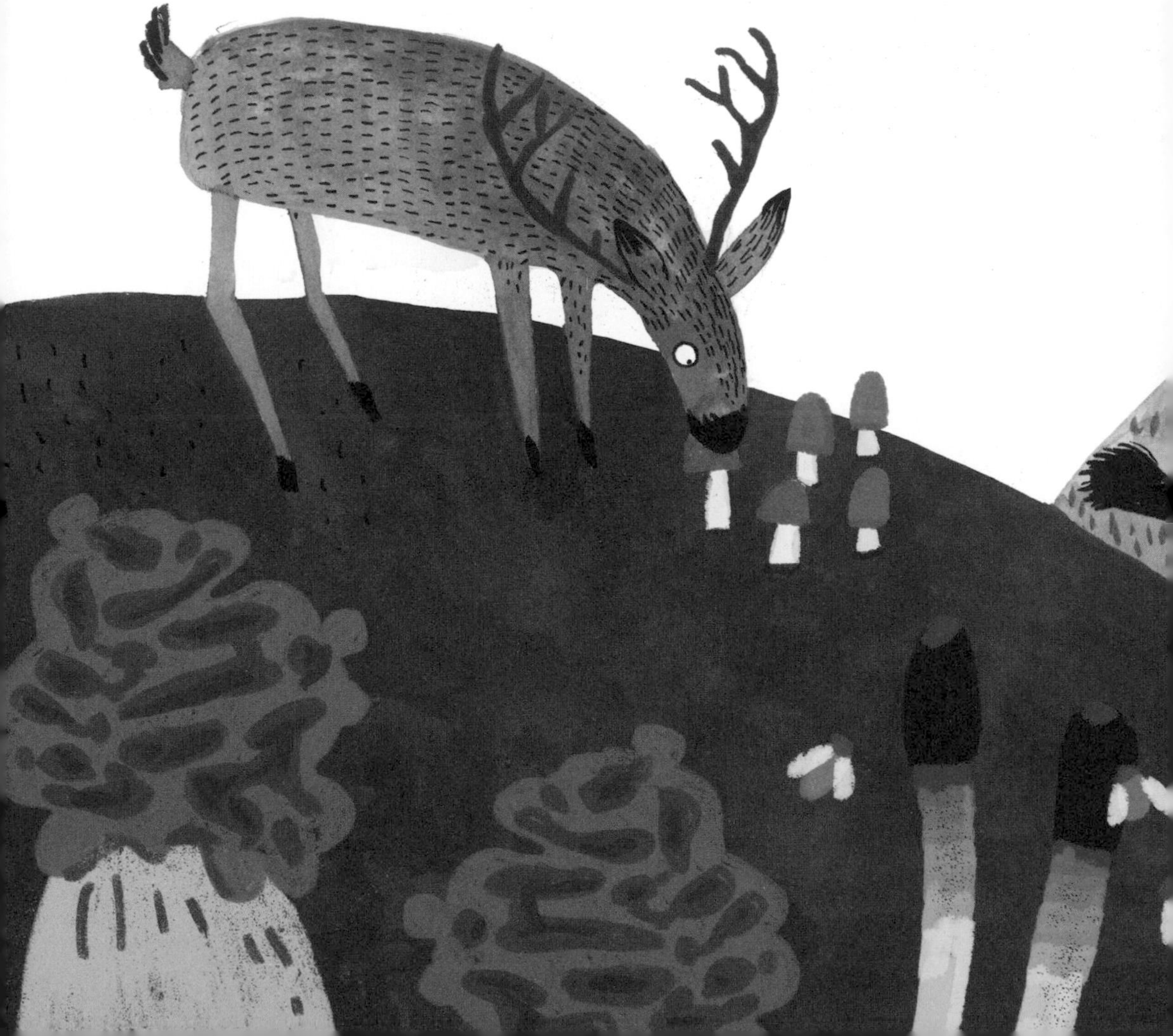

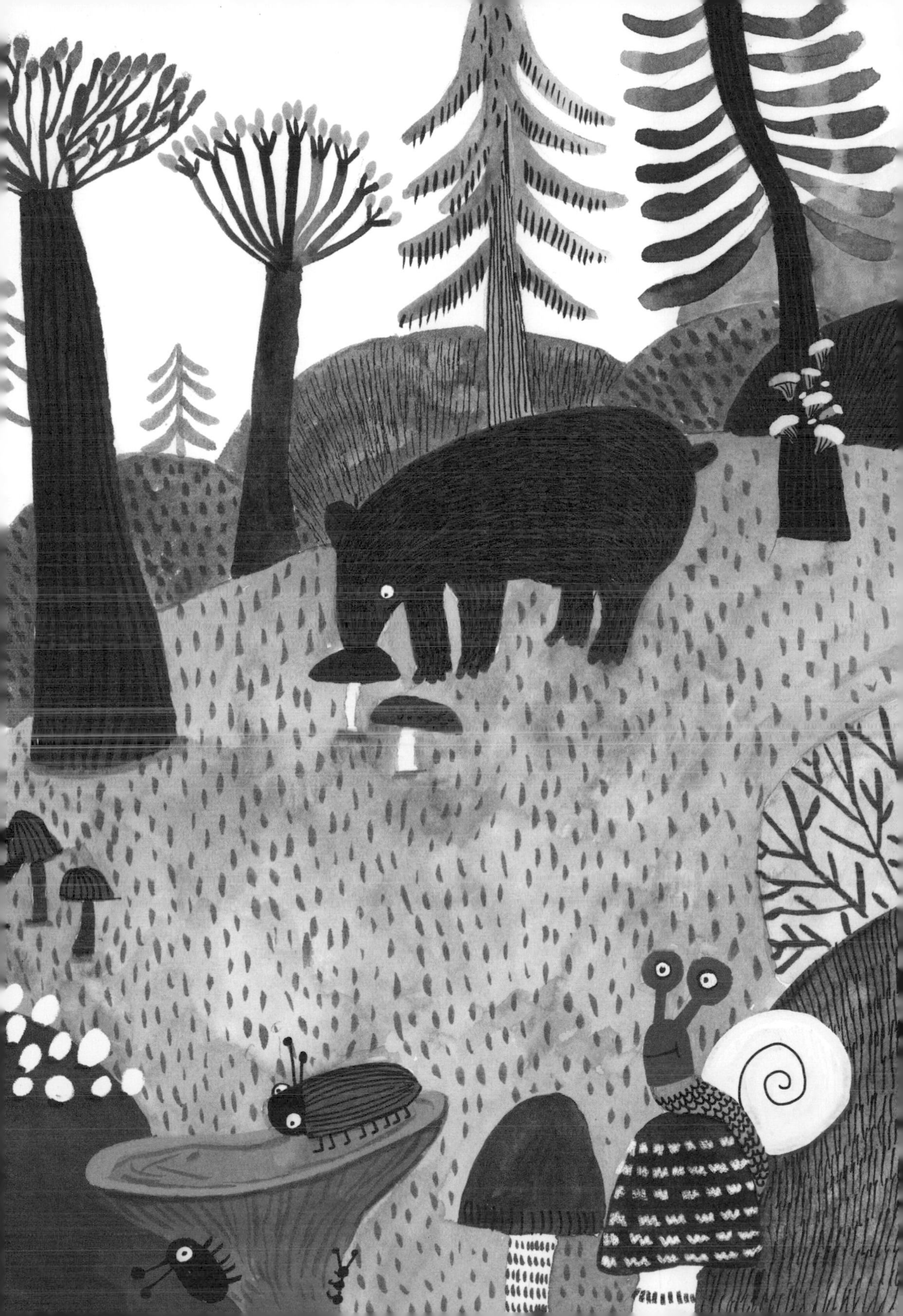

Would you like to come for a walk with us? I'll introduce you to some of my mushroom buddies. But first, I'd like you to follow these two rules:

⭐1 PROTECT THEIR ENVIRONMENT

Mushrooms are often friends with the plants in the forest, helping them and many animals survive. So be gentle and don't litter. And try not to pick too many mushrooms: leave some for the slugs and squirrels!

And you know, you can always draw a picture of the mushrooms you find, or even take a photo.

2 DON'T EAT THEM!

Many mushrooms are poisonous. Only grown-up mycologists know for certain which ones are safe to eat.

WE CAN MAKE YOU VERY, VERY SICK!
AND EVEN WORSE!

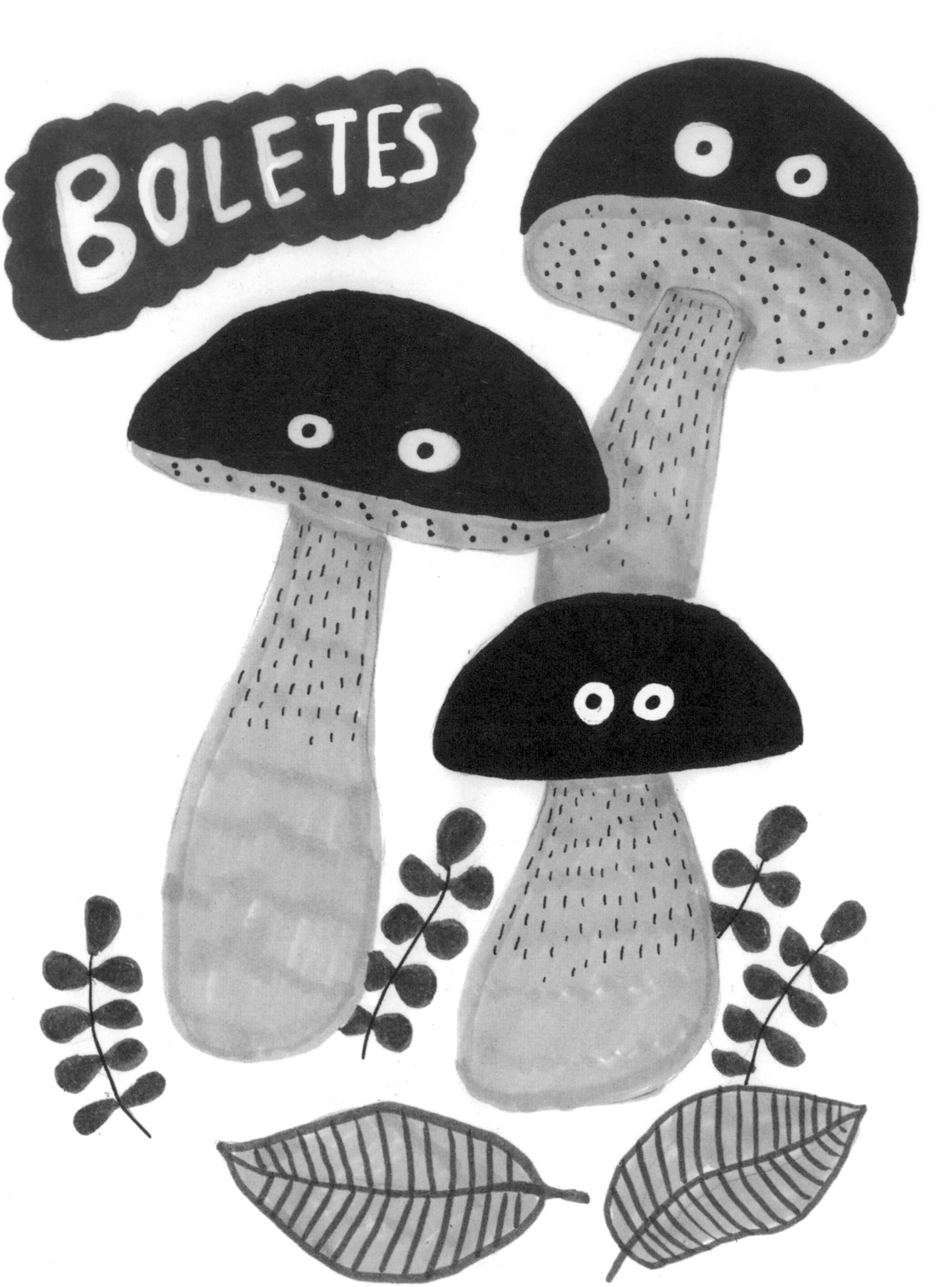
BOLETES

If you find a mushroom with sponge-like holes under its cap, it might be a bolete. There are many species of boletes, and some are delicious! You can find dried boletes in grocery stores.

Some boletes turn blue when we touch them. It's very pretty.

Others have a slimy cap, like a slug. And some have spots that look like dragon scales.

Bugs like boletes a lot, so these mushrooms are often home to hundreds of tiny worms!

THE Chanterelle

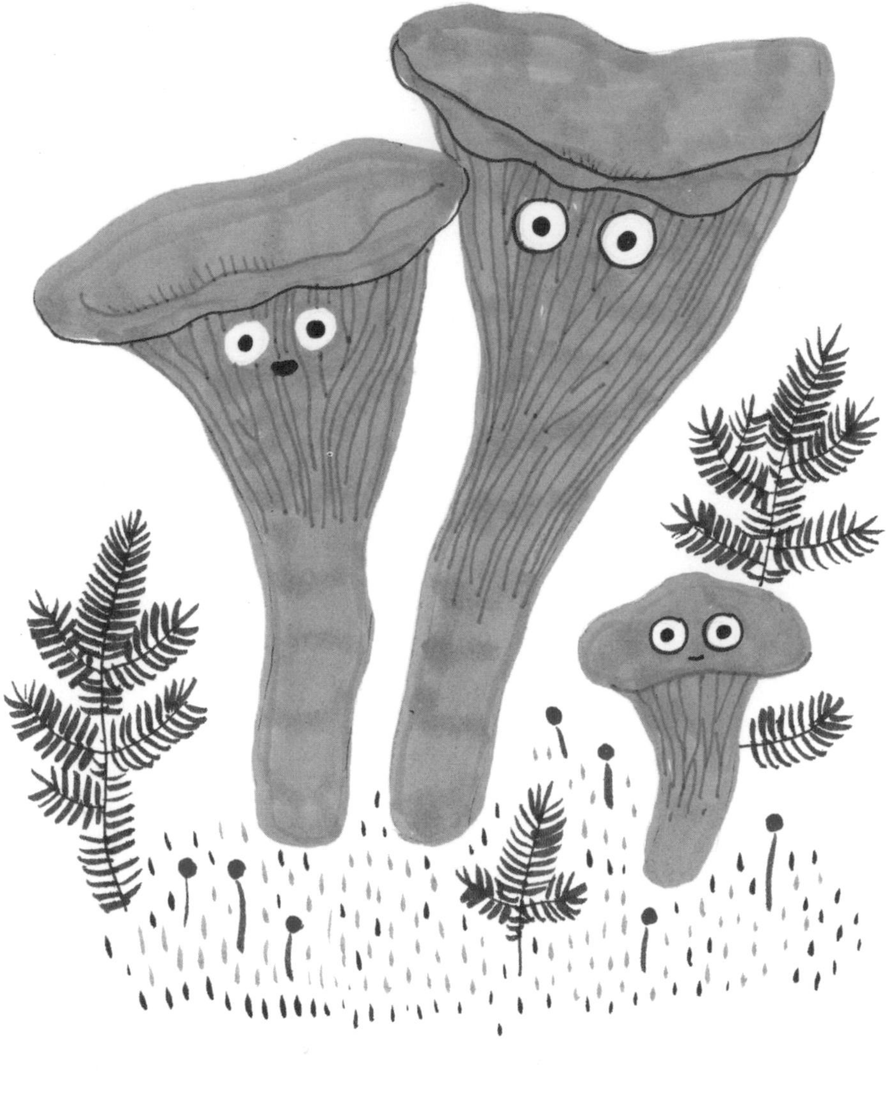

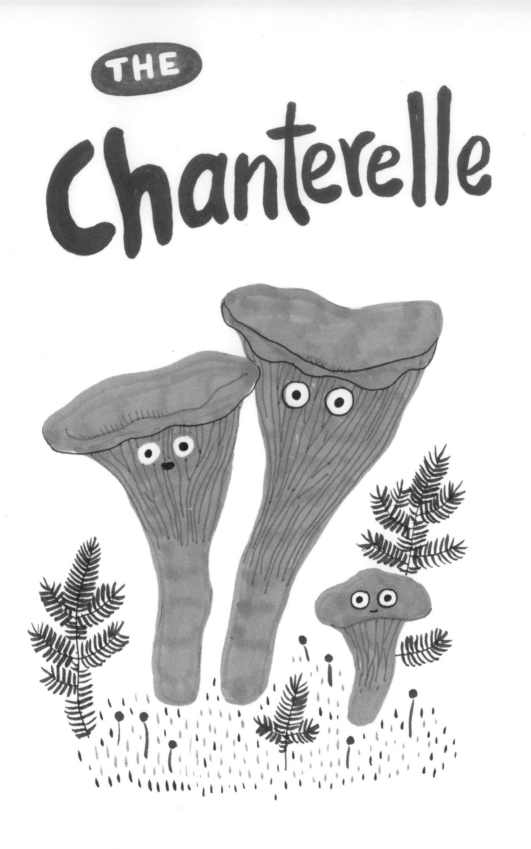

The chanterelle is one of the first mushrooms
I learned to identify. They're very pretty, bright
orange, and often grow with a bunch of friends.

They're easy to recognize because their caps look
like a trumpet. Instead of gills, they have little
folds, like an old person's wrinkles.

Some mushrooms look like chanterelles but
are very toxic. They are called jack o'lantern
mushrooms. It's a pretty name, don't you think?

The main difference between them is jack
o'lantern mushrooms have real gills instead
of wrinkles.

Aaaah, morels. They are so cute. They look like an alien's brain.

I love morels, and when I find some, I jump all over the place and squeal. It's silly, but I can't help myself. It's because I don't find them often!

Morels like to grow where there have been forest fires. They love the ashes.

They're hard to see because they look like the dead leaves they grow on, or like pine cones. They are hide-and-seek champions.

THE MOREL

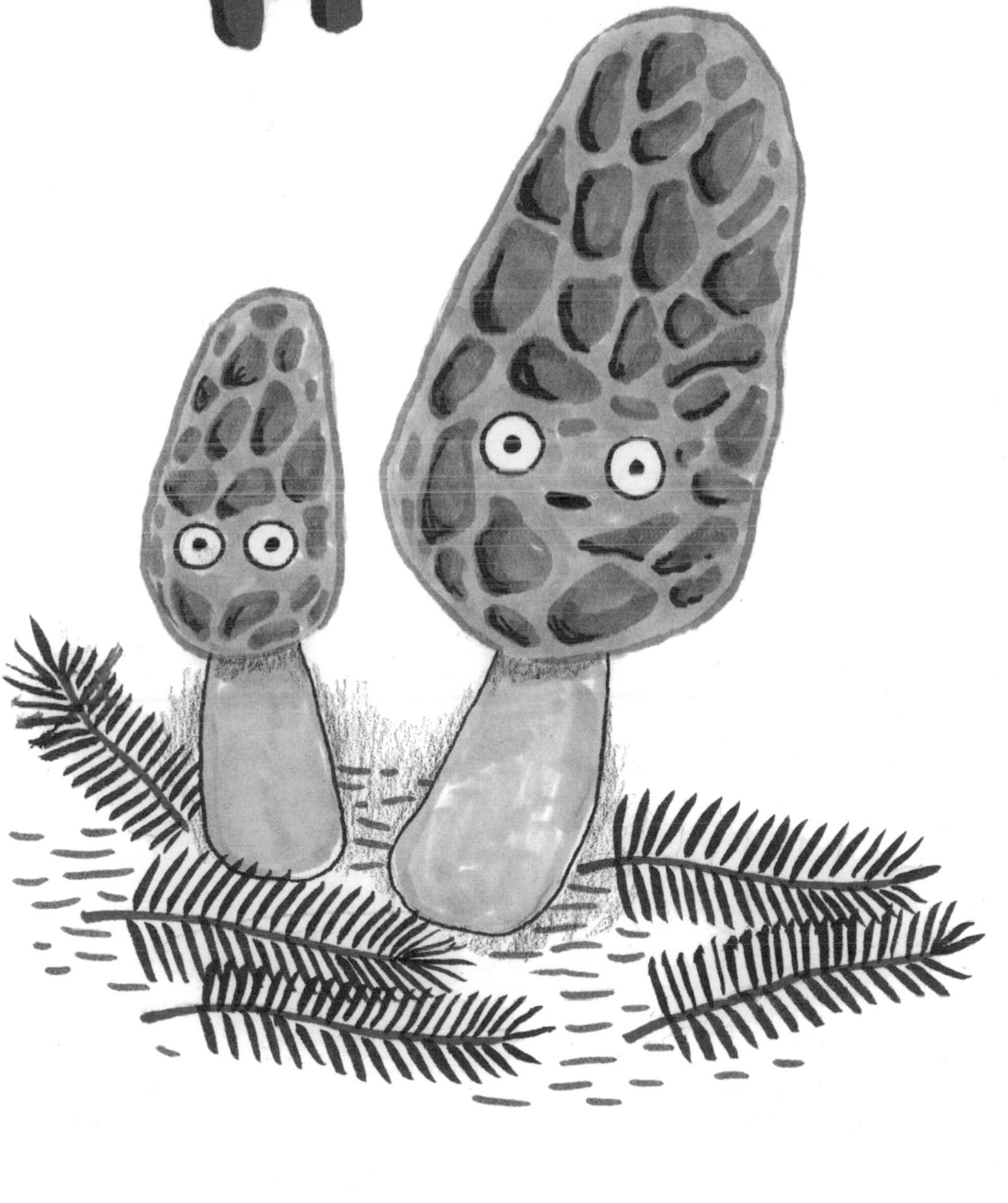

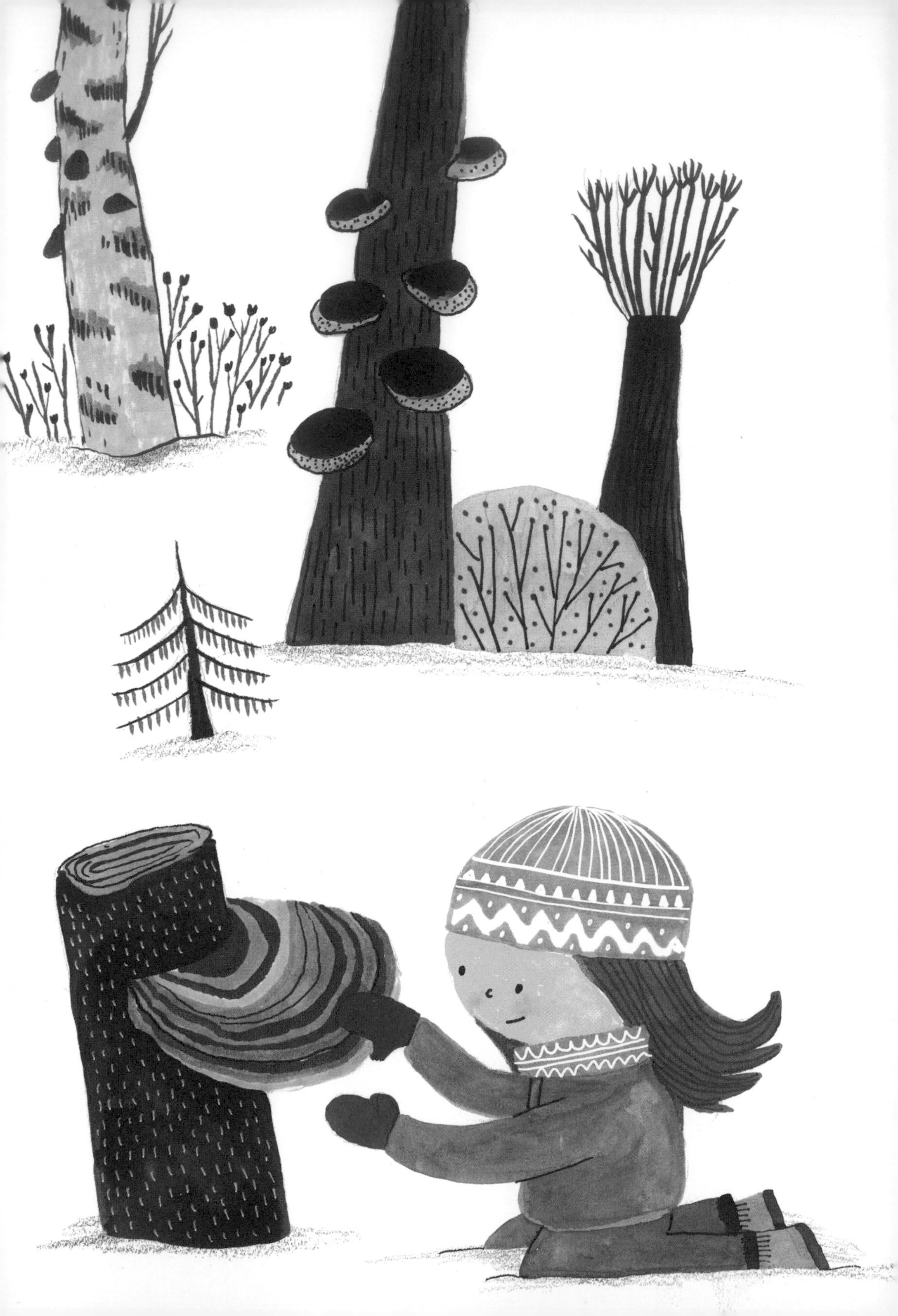

My daughters' favourite mushrooms are

POLYPORES.

These hard mushrooms often grow on tree trunks or roots and can get pretty big. My oldest daughter collects them. We once found one as big as a plate! These mushrooms are cool because you can find them even in the winter.

THE False Morel

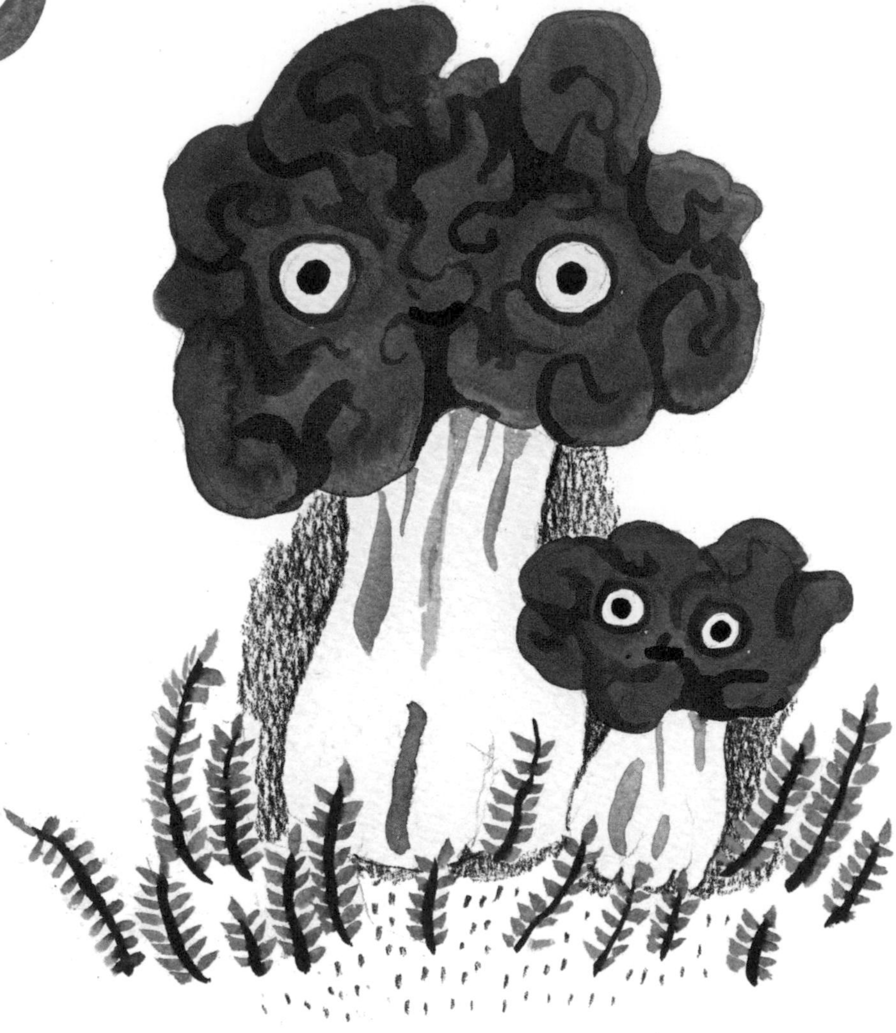

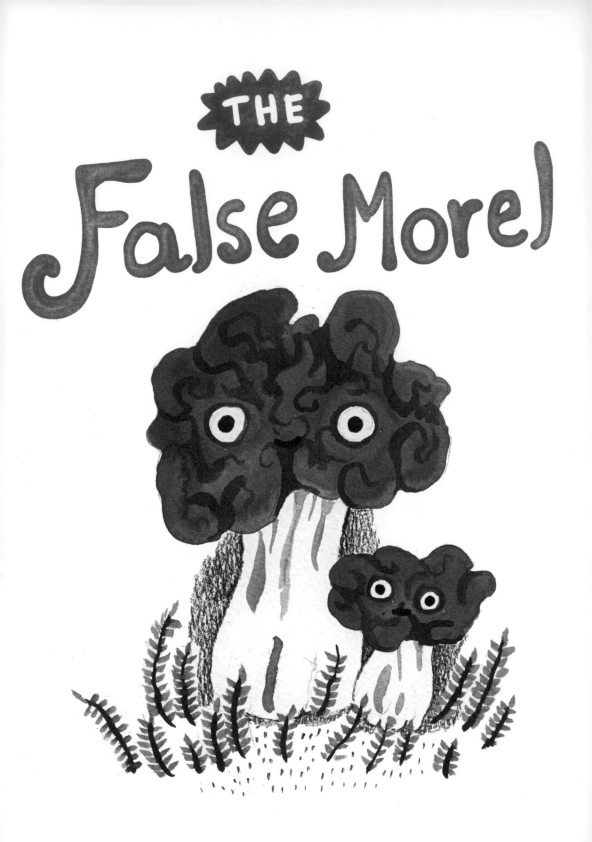

Here's another guy that looks like a brain. Its latin name is gyromitra. Since it looks a bit like a morel, it's sometimes called a false morel.

When you touch it, it feels like cold rubber, and there are lots of little caves inside its cap!

If I were a bug, I'd like my house to be inside a gyromitra.

Some mushrooms produce a liquid that looks like milk when you cut them. We call these lactarius mushrooms.

The lactarius indigo is special because the milk it produces is bright blue.

I've never found any, but I keep looking. I think they're quite rare!

If you see one, you're lucky. I'll be jealous and insist you take me mushroom hunting with you next time!

THE LACTARIUS INDIGO

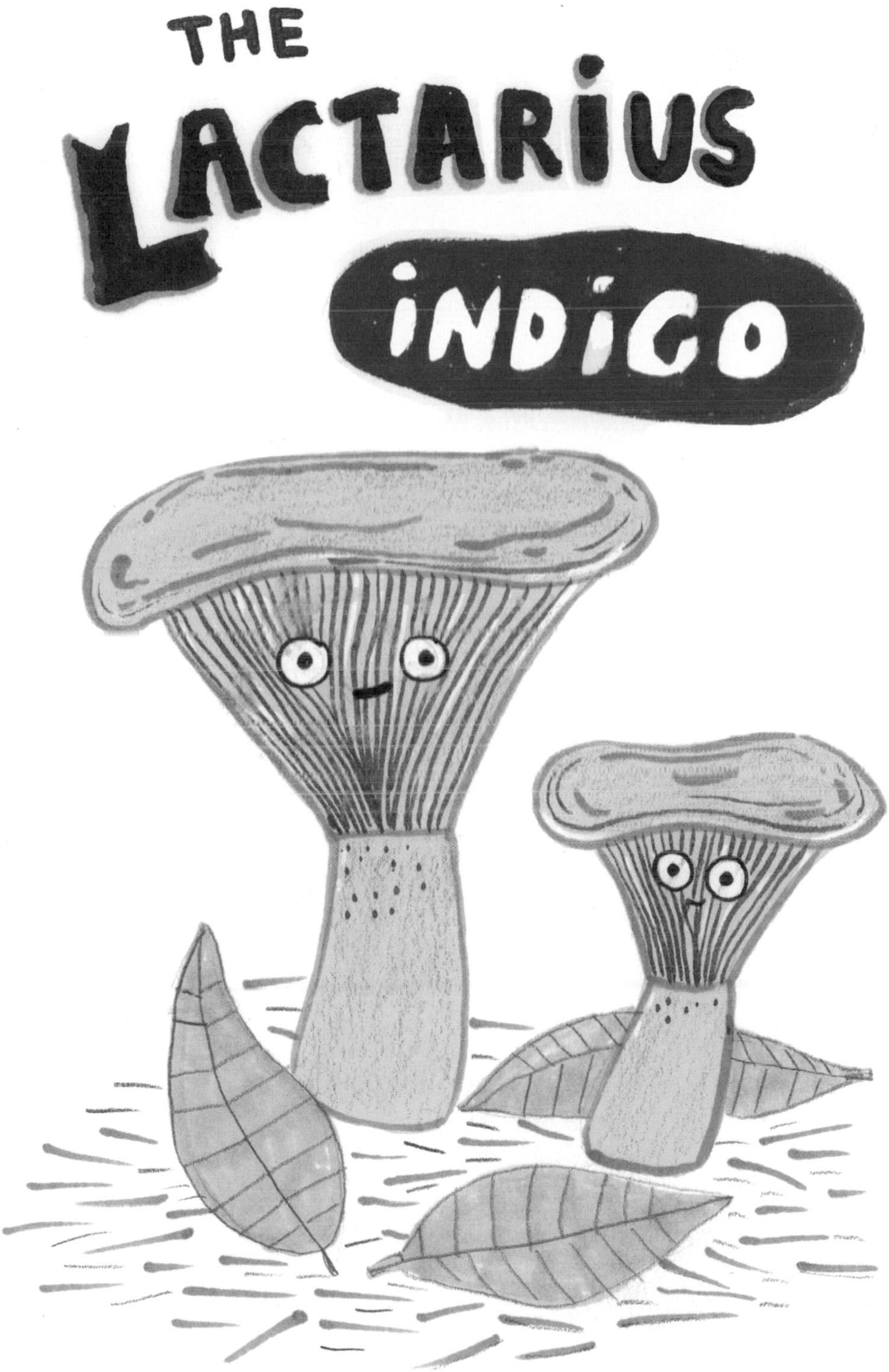

THE PUFFBALL

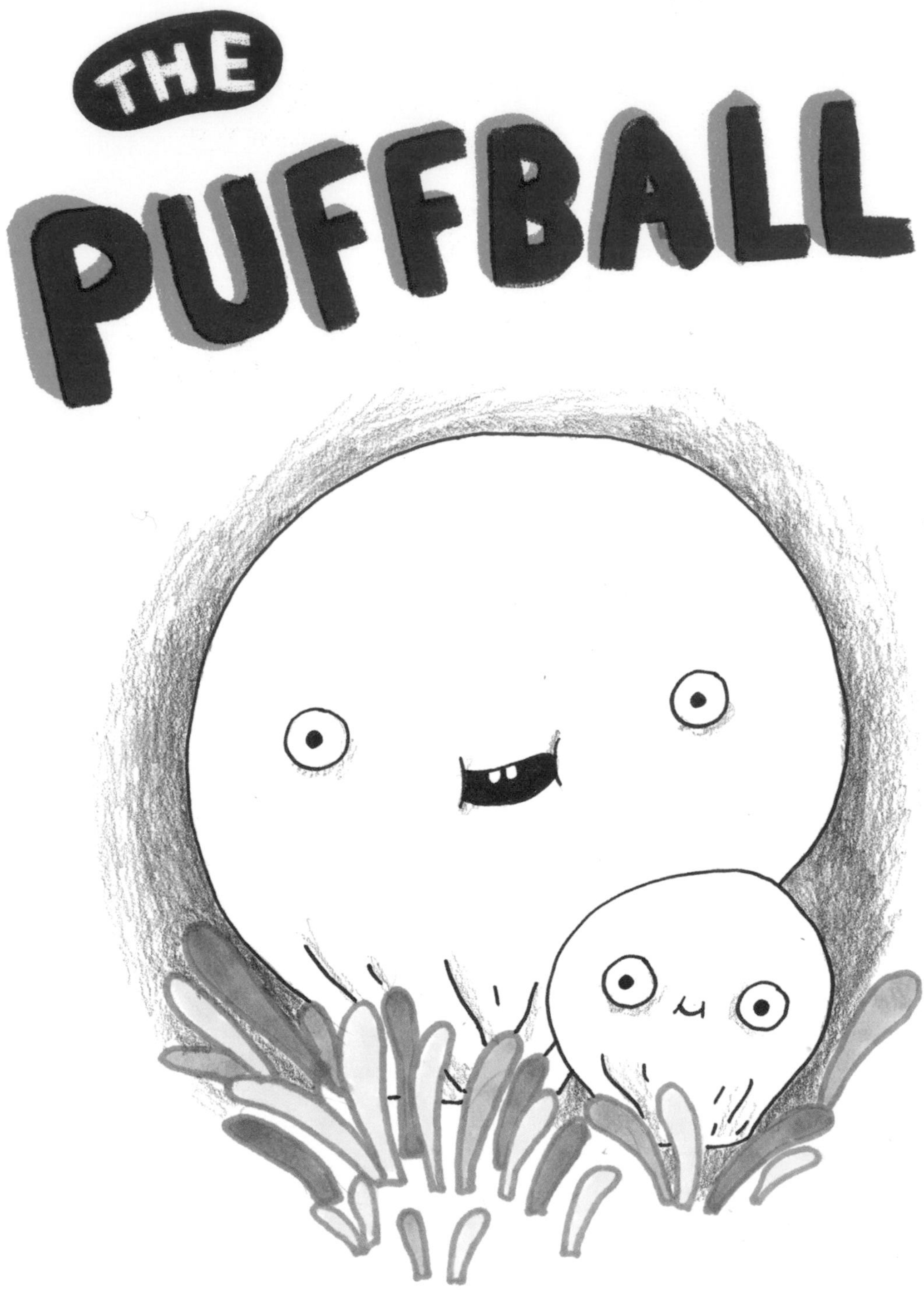

The puffball is an interesting specimen. When it's young, it's all white and smooth, like an egg or a golfball.

Then, as it grows up, it turns yellow or brown or grey, and then something funny happens: if you step on it, POOF! It bursts into a cloud of smoke, like a cartoon fart.

It's their way of freeing their spores.

Elegant, isn't it?

Some of them are HUGE, like basketballs. We call them giant puffballs.

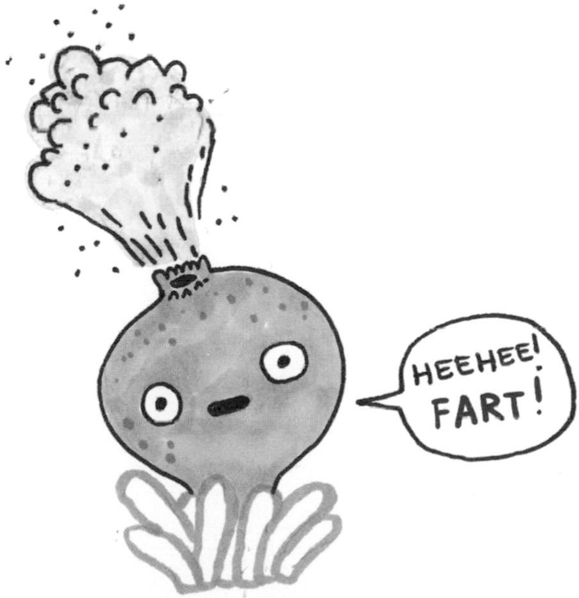
HEEHEE! FART!

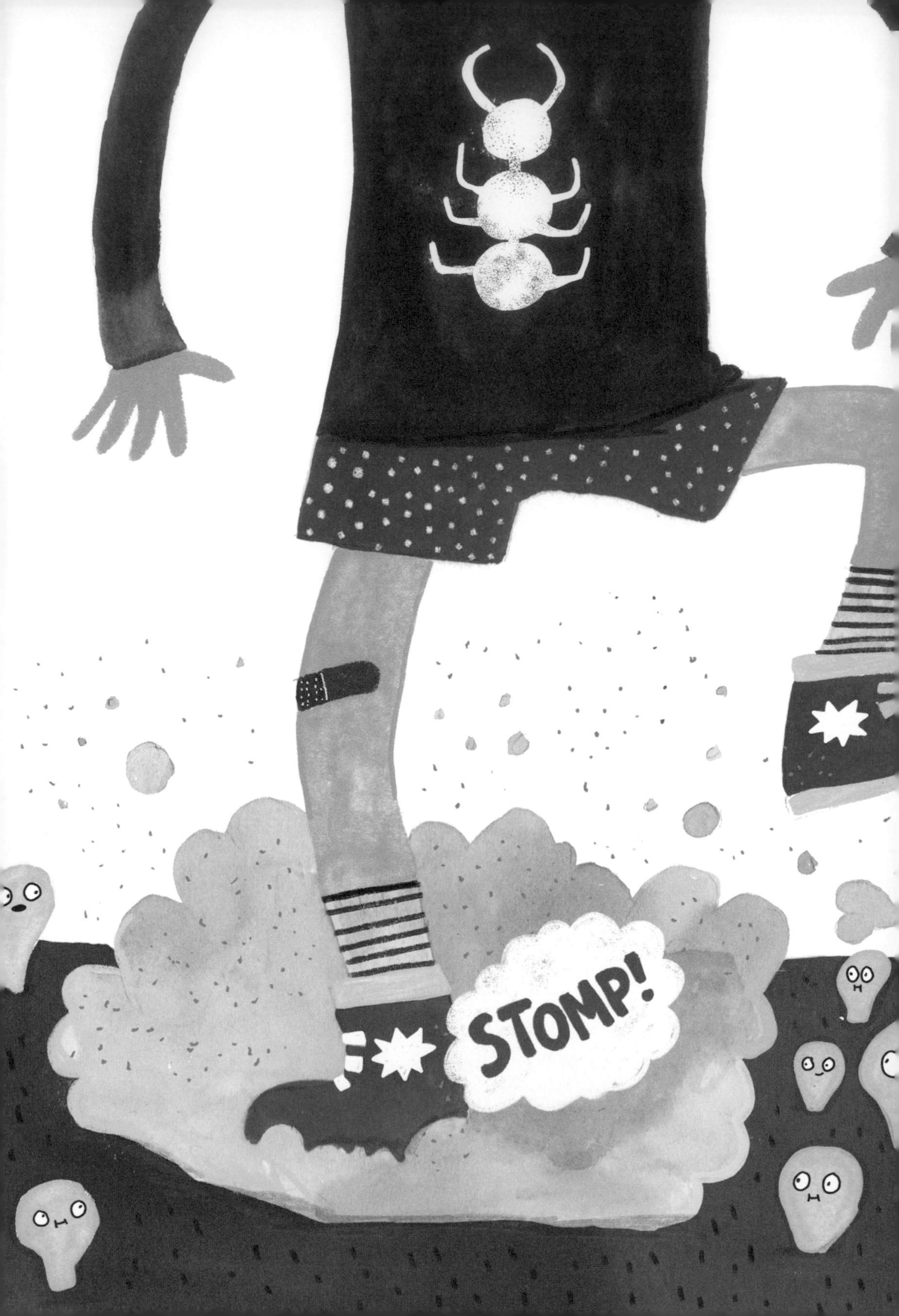
STOMP!

I'm taking a little break from sharing facts to draw my daughter stepping on puffballs. It's too fun!

I know, I said not to destroy mushrooms, but no need to worry about the puffballs. They like it when you step on them! It makes their spores go everywhere, which helps them reproduce.

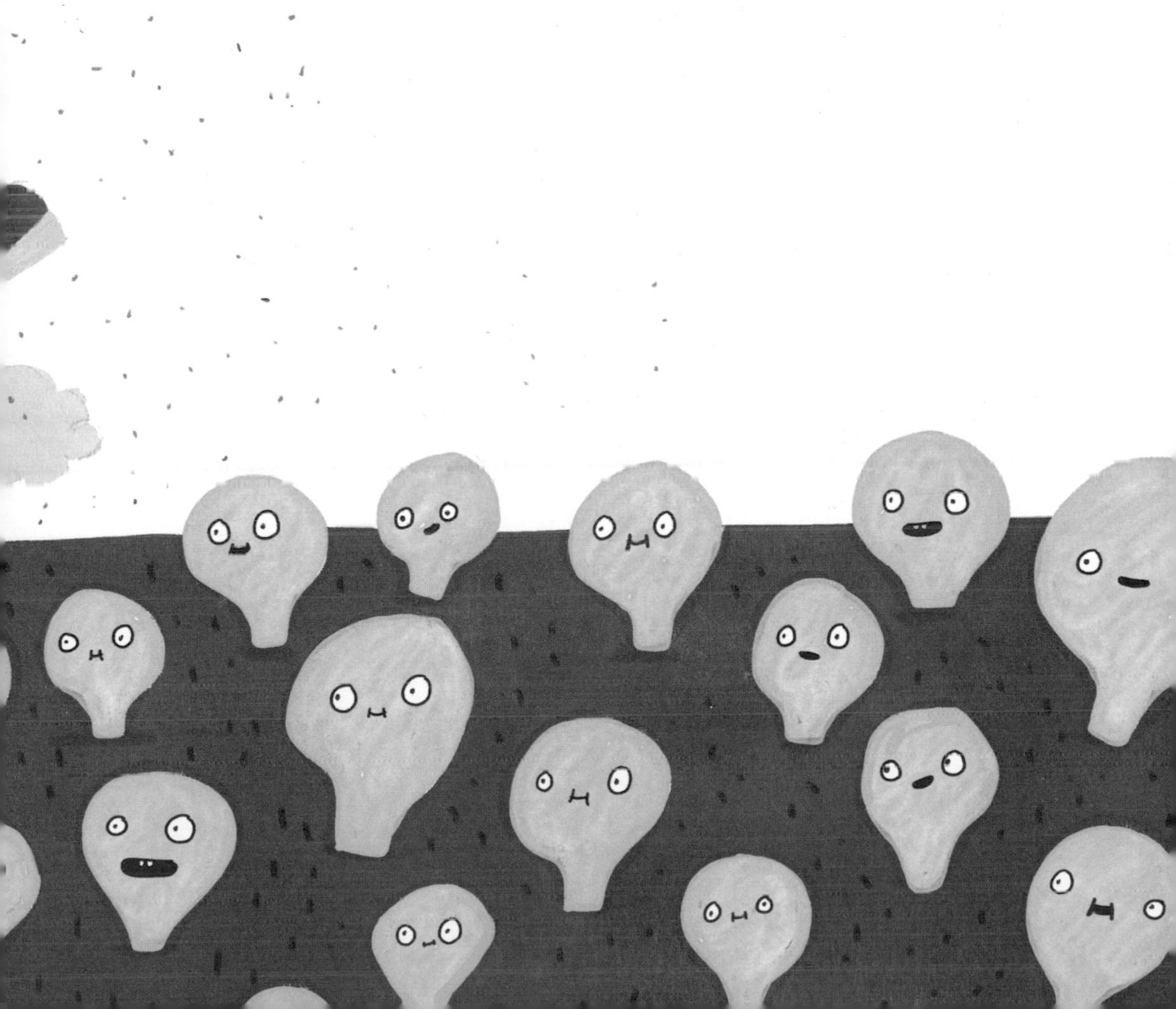

THE
CORAL MUSHROOM

I really like this one. It looks like something that would grow at the bottom of the sea. That's why they're called coral mushrooms.

Some are grey or white or pink, but this one is my favourite. I've seen very big ones!

Instead of a cap, it has many fingers that point to the sky.

They're very fragile; be gentle with them!

THE FLY AGARIC

The fly agaric is a very pretty mushroom.
I find them all the time. Their caps are red
or yellow, depending on where in the world
you find them!

Illustrators (like me) love to draw them in
picture books: they're so handsome!

When they grow, the fly agaric comes out
of something that looks like an egg.

We call it fly agaric because, a long time ago,
people would crush them in milk to repel flies.

They're very pretty, but don't eat them. They're

THE DOG STINKHORN

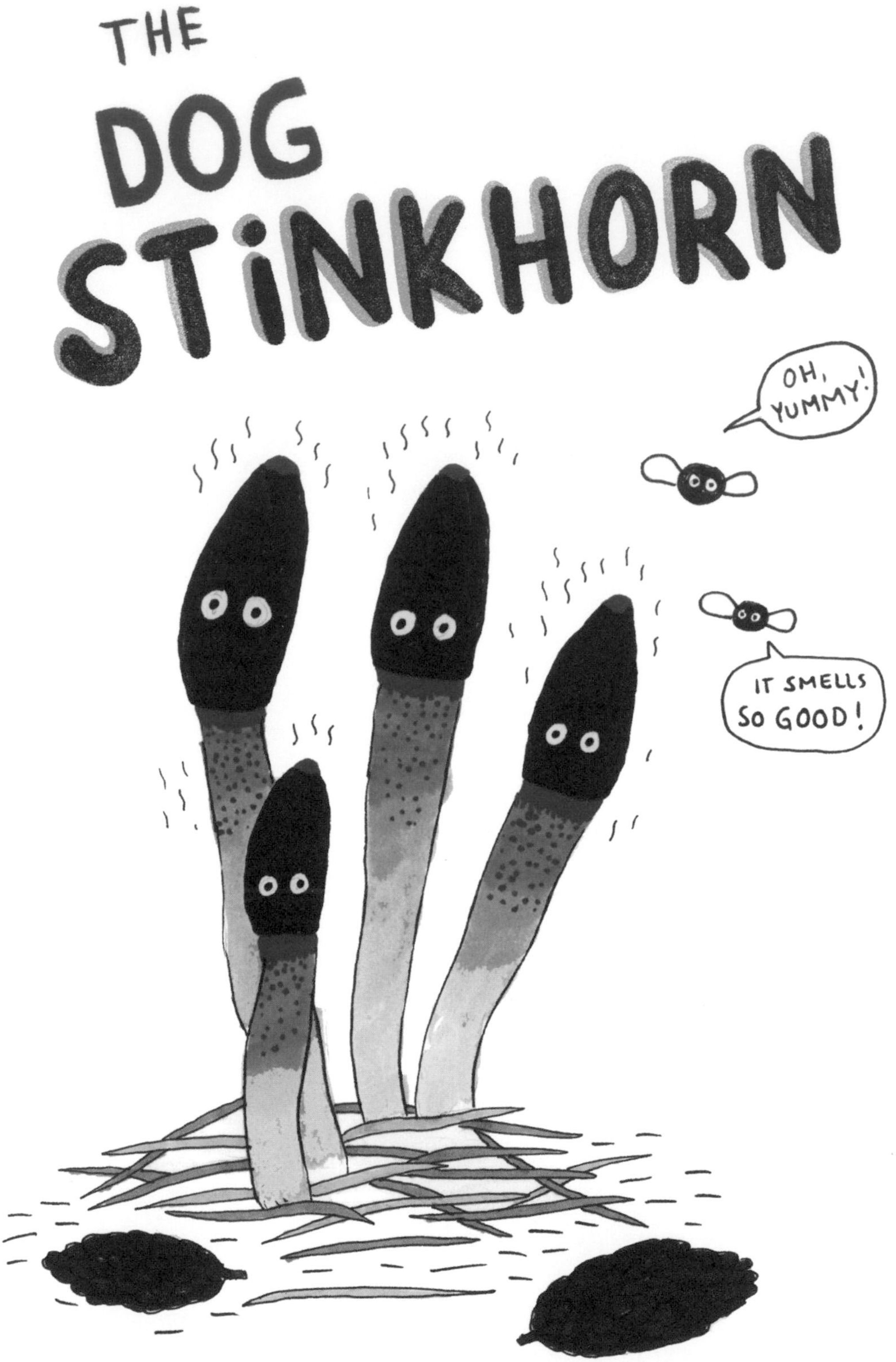
OH, YUMMY!
IT SMELLS SO GOOD!

These guys are the kings of the stinkers.
They smell like dog poop. The smell is so strong
that sometimes you smell them even before
you see them.

They stink like this to attract flies, who help
them disperse their spores.

I've seen some in a park near my house,
and believe me, you don't want to eat them.

Unless you're a fly, of course.

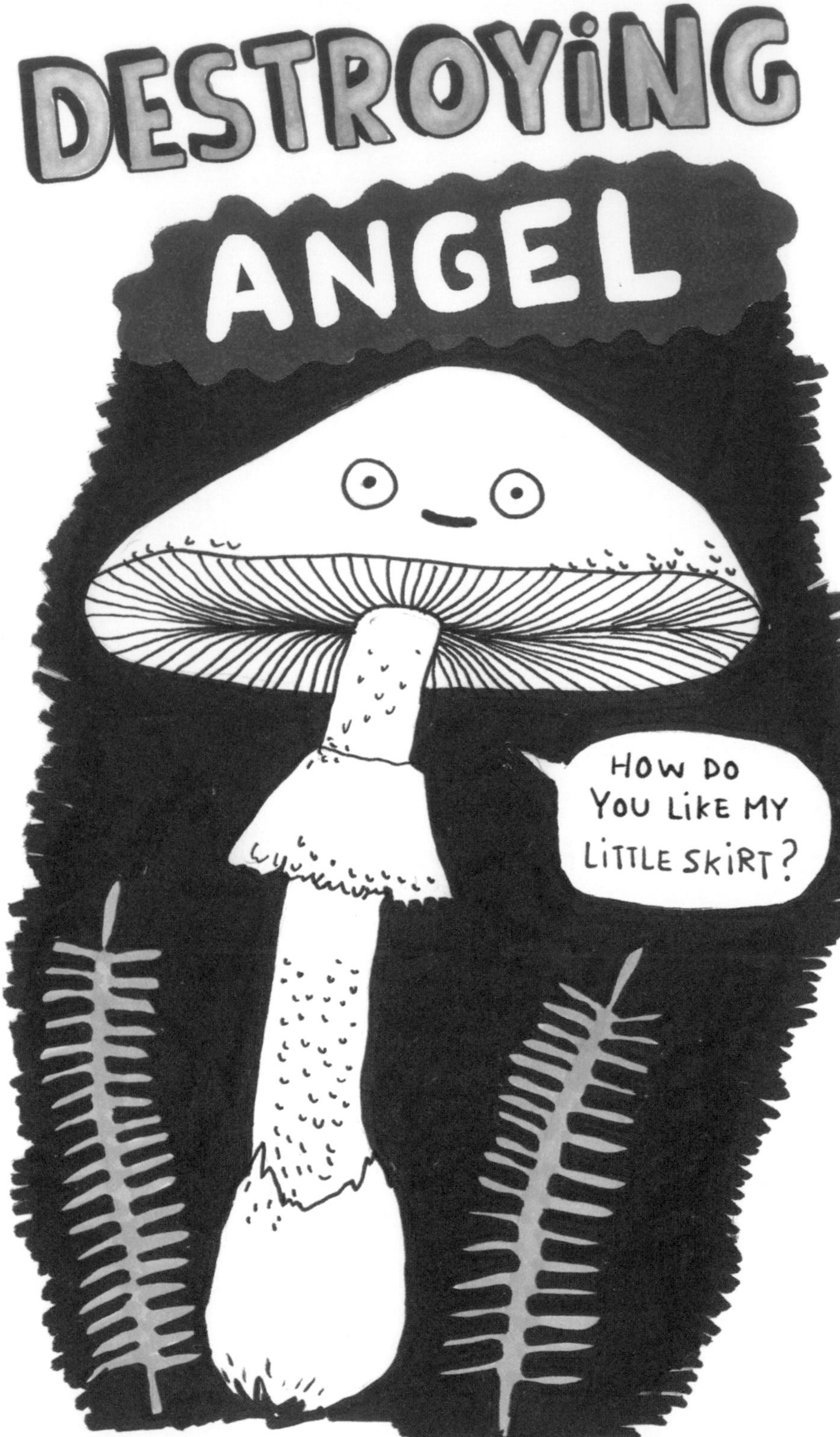
DESTROYiNG
ANGEL
HOW DO YOU LIKE MY LITTLE SKIRT?

Oooooh, Amanita virosa! Everytime I see one, I get chills.

It's because it's one of the most toxic mushrooms: it can even be deadly.

It's sometimes called a destroying angel. To me, it looks like a ghost.

So, this one? Don't touch it, all right?

As I was saying earlier, there are so many species of mushrooms! I wish I could tell you about all of them, but that would be a very long book!

Instead, I'll tell you about the beautiful mushroom names I've come across.

Just listen to those names! How poetic! They sound like the ingredients for a witch's spell.

PINK DISCO

DRAB TOOTH

GOLDEN NAVEL

THE PRETENDER

WET ROT

GASSY WEBCAP

DEWDROP DAPPERLING

INK CAP

BUG SPUTNIK

CINNAMON JELLYBABY

BIRD'S NEST FUNGI

FUNERAL BELL

CAT DAPPERLING

BALD KNIGHT

WITCHES' BUTTER

BITTER POISONPIE

JACK O'LANTERN

LION SHIELD

MEALY OYSTER

VAMPIRE'S BANE

CABBAGE PARACHUTE

POTATO EARTHBALL

PLUMS AND CUSTARD

DEAD MOLL'S FINGERS

HOTLIPS

ELBOWPATCH CRUST

WHISKERY MILKCAP

KING ALFRED'S CAKE

TIGER'S EYE

TURQUOISE ELFCUP

DRUMSTICK TRUFFLECLUB

DEVIL'S FINGERS

POWDERY PIGGYBACK

When we come back from our walks, we put our treasures on the table and look in our books to try to identify them all.

It's hard! So many of them look alike!

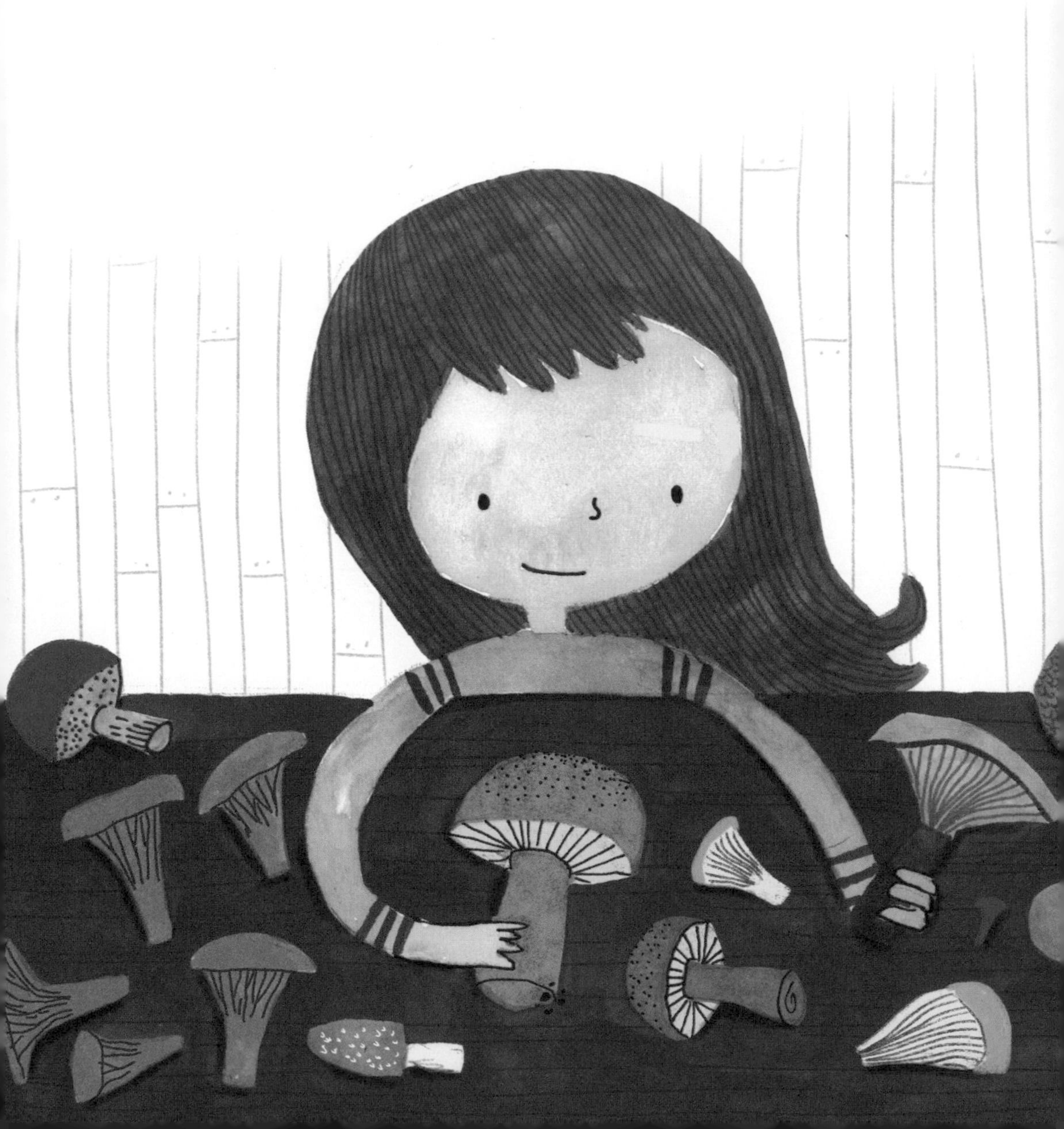

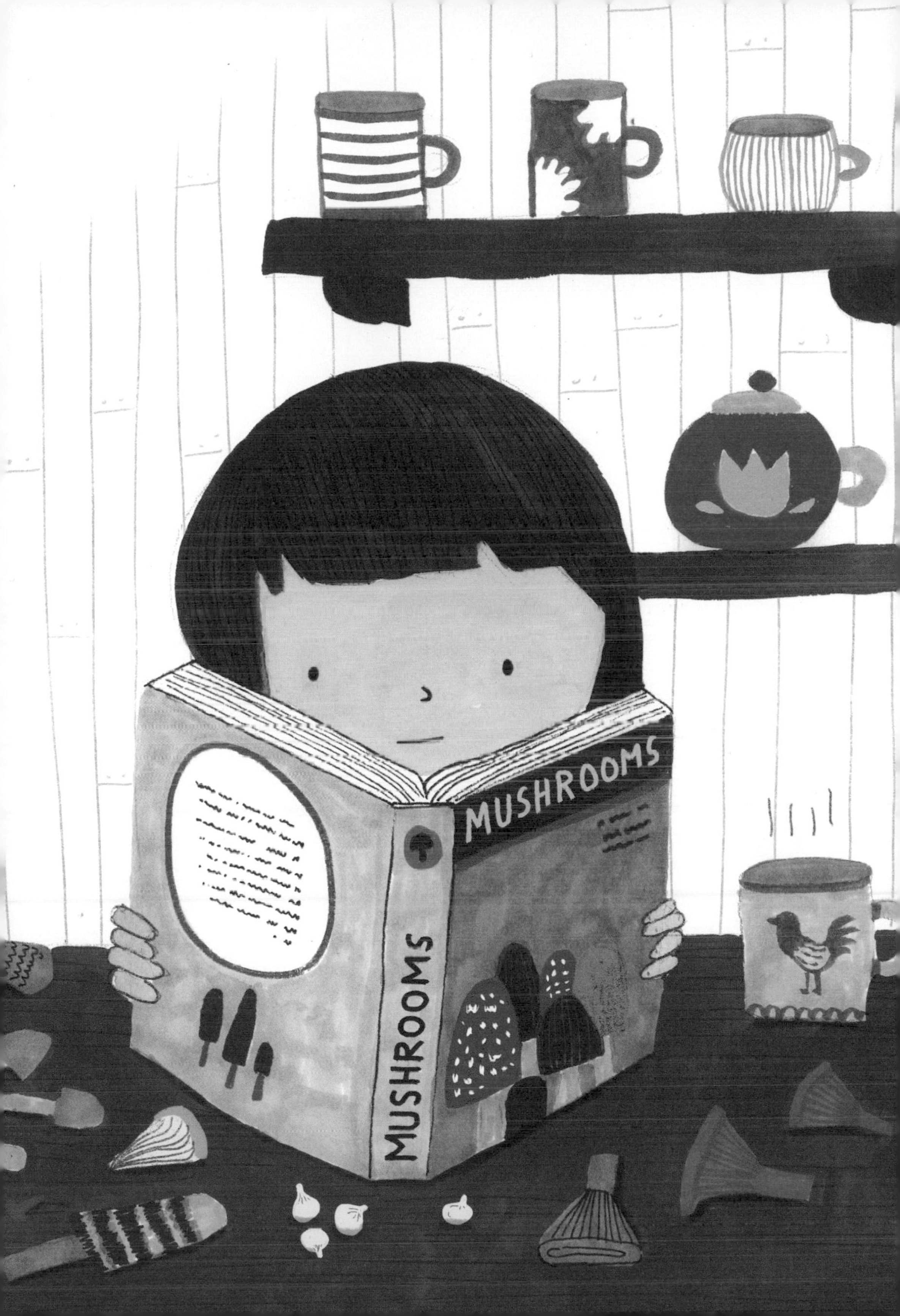
MUSHROOMS
MUSHROOMS

So, did you enjoy our

TREASURE HUNT?

Would you like to find out more about mushrooms?

There are many books about fungi where you'll discover wonders I don't even know about. Check them out at your local library!

And don't forget to take lots of walks in the woods.

Have fun now!

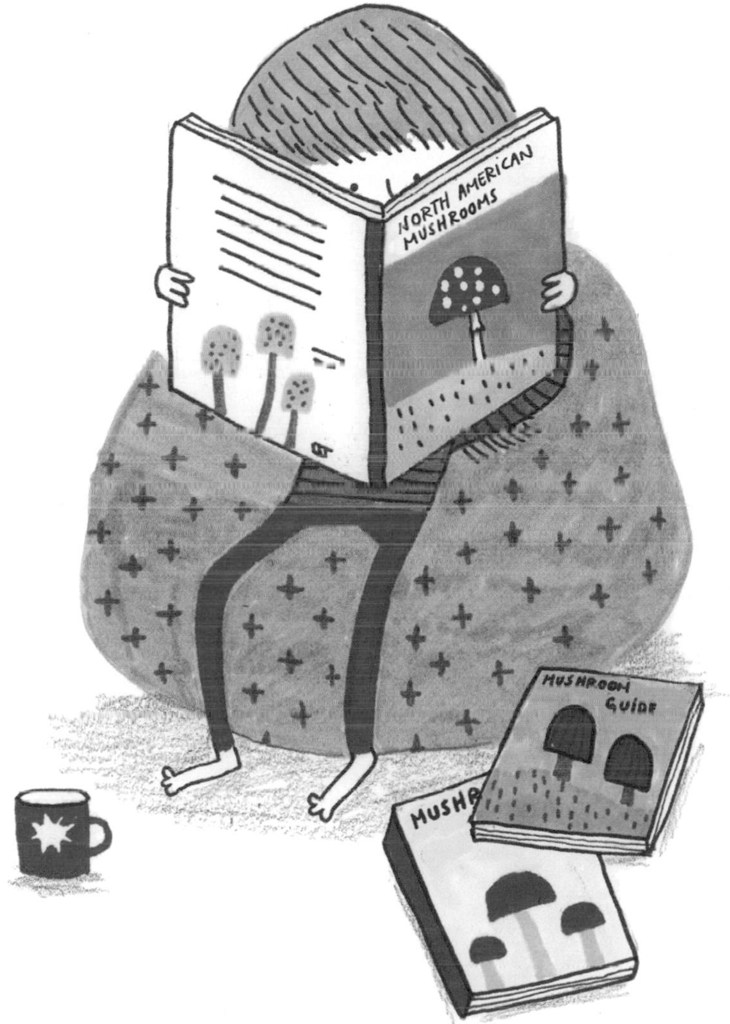
NORTH AMERICAN
MUSHROOMS
MUSHROOM
GUIDE
MUSH

MUSHROOM

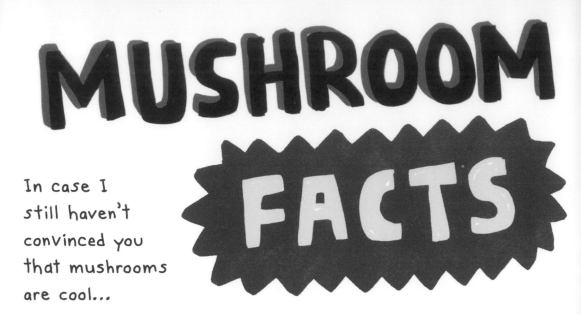

FACTS

In case I still haven't convinced you that mushrooms are cool...

There are about thirty species of mushrooms that glow in the dark!

The super mushroom from Mario is the poisonous fly agaric.

KRAAK!

POP! POP! POP! POP!

Mushrooms grow better where lightning has recently struck.

This mushroom, called sulphur shelf, grows on trees and tastes almost exactly like fried chicken.

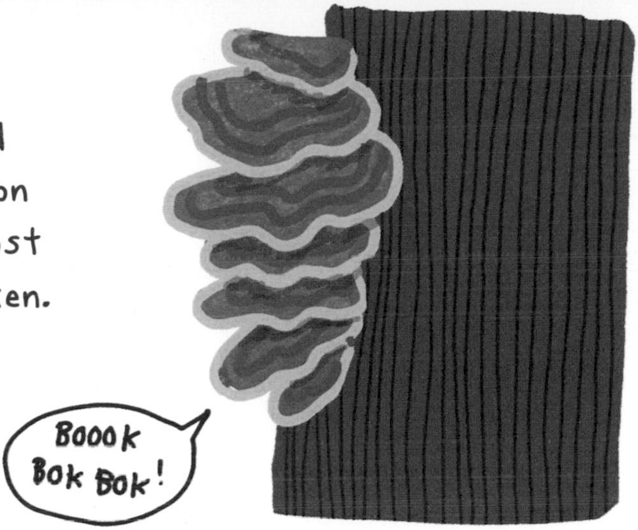
Booo k
Bok Bok!

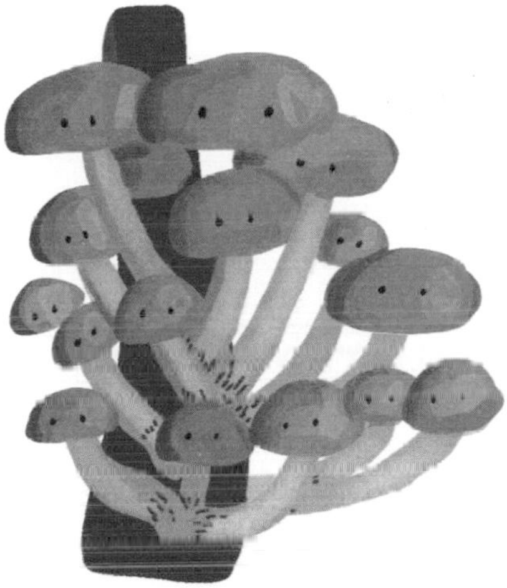

In Oregon, there is a mushroom that is 2400 years old. Its mycelium (the underground part of the mushroom) covers a surface bigger than a soccer field. It's destroying thousands of trees.

Mushrooms can be used to make:

Bread
Beer
Medication
Fabric and wool dye
Bricks
Fake leather
Cheese
and much more!

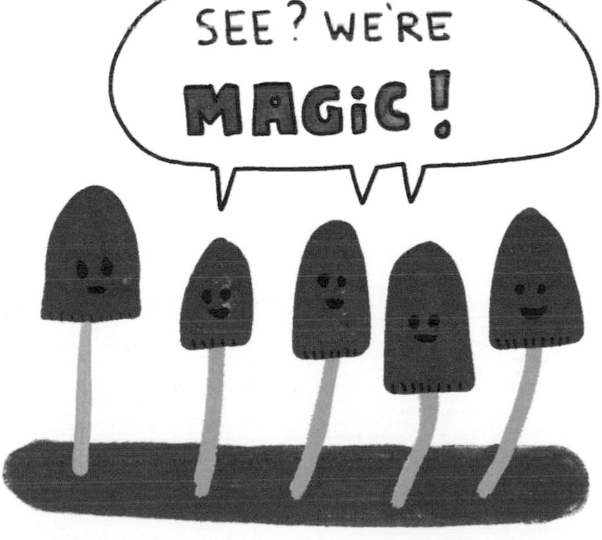
SEE? WE'RE
MAGIC!

that happened to me while hunting

MUSHROOMS:

Found a moose skull

Scared a snake

Came face to face with a porcupine

Found a giant bear poop

Met a baby deer

Walked on a wasp's nest (ouch!)

Walked into poison ivy (double ouch!)

Met nice people and made new friends

Mushroom hunting is a big

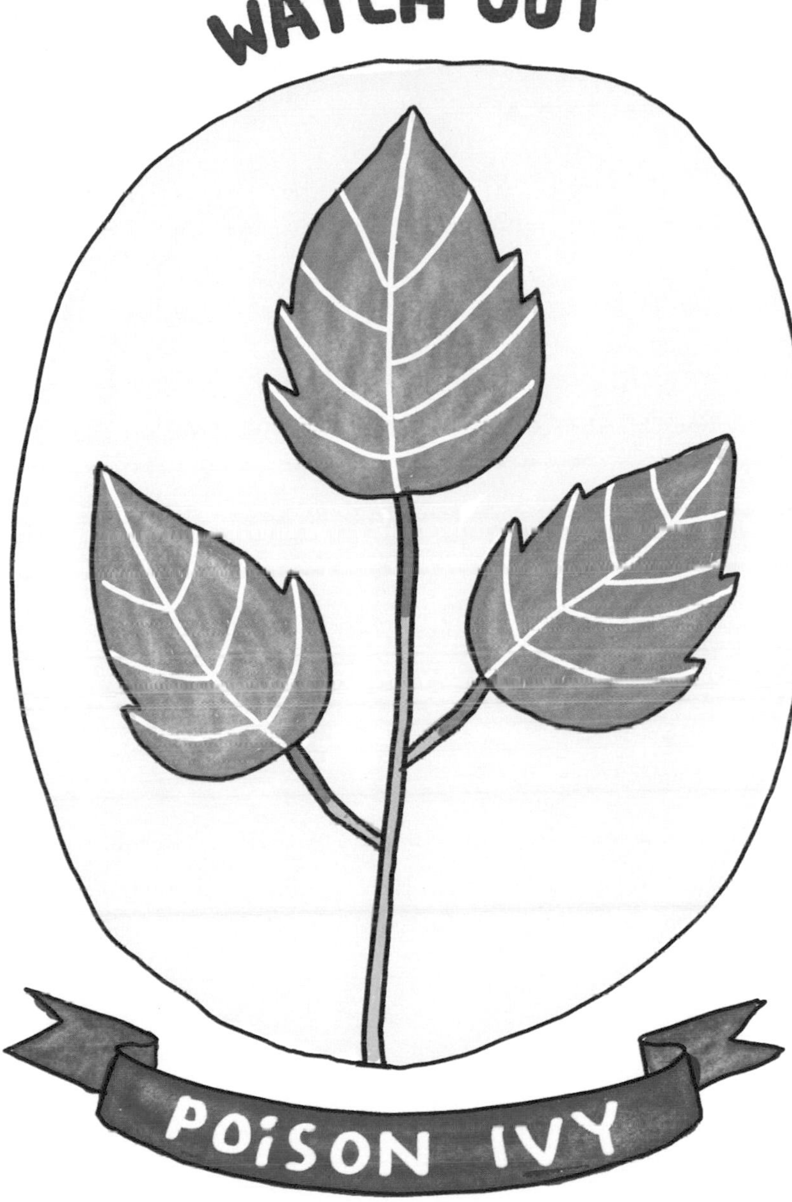
WATCH OUT
POISON IVY

HOW TO DO A SPORE PRINT

Spore prints are very pretty, and the colour of the spores can even help you identify the mushrooms!

You will need:

1 A MUSHROOM

2 SOME PAPER

3 A GLASS OR BOWL

(A glass for small mushrooms, a bowl for bigger ones.)

1. Remove the stem; you only need the cap.

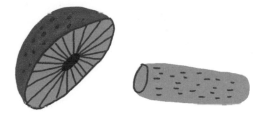

2. Put the mushroom cap on a piece of paper with the tubes or gills facing down. Cover it with a glass or a bowl.

3. Let it sit all night. In the morning, you should see a pretty spore print. If you can't see anything, it's because the spores are the same colour as your paper! You can decorate them too, like I did!

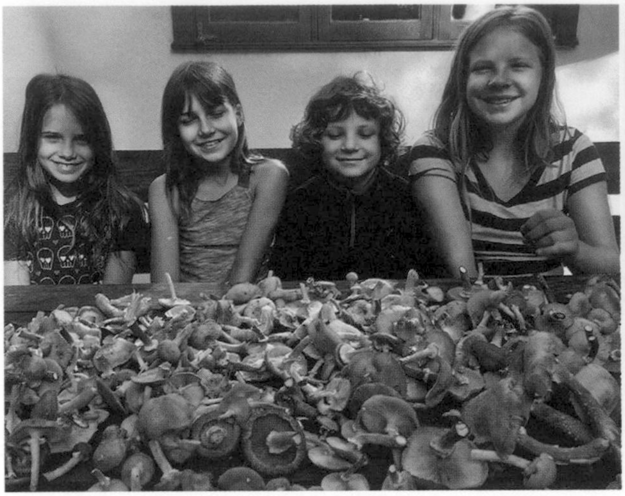

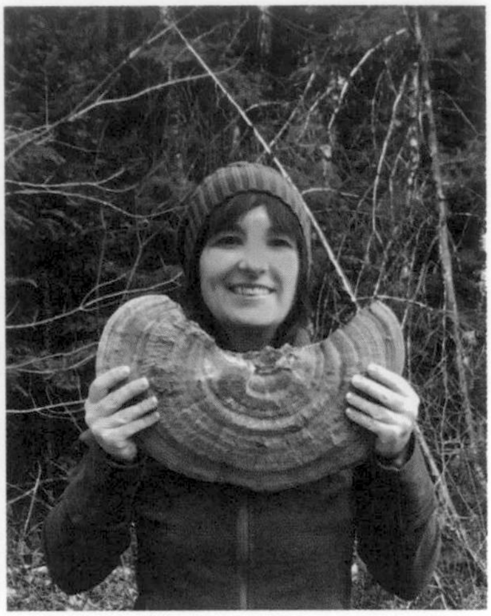

My daughters and their friends and I posing with some of the mushrooms we found on our many walks!

For Philo, Émile, Albert, and Lydie,
my best mushroom-hunting buddies

Thank you to The Mycoboutique in Montreal for sharing their mushroom expertise and helping me to get all my mushroom facts in order.

drawnandquarterly.com | elisegravel.com

ISBN 978-1-77046-322-6
First edition: June 2018 | Second printing: October 2018 | Third printing: May 2019 |
Fourth printing: December 2019 | Fifth printing: November 2020 | Sixth printing: December 2021
Seventh printing: July 2023
Printed in China | 10 9 8 7

Cataloguing data available from Library and Archives Canada.

Published in the USA by Drawn & Quarterly, a client publisher of Farrar, Straus and Giroux.
Published in Canada by Drawn & Quarterly, a client publisher of Raincoast Books.
Published in the United Kingdom by Drawn & Quarterly, a client publisher of Publishers Group UK.

Canada Drawn & Quarterly acknowledges the support of the Government of Canada and the Canada Council for the Arts for our publishing program.

Drawn & Quarterly reconnaît l'aide financière du gouvernement du Québec par l'entremise de la Société de développement des entreprises culturelles (SODEC) pour nos activités d'édition.
Gouvernement du Québec—Programme de crédit d'impôt pour l'édition de livres—Gestion SODEC.

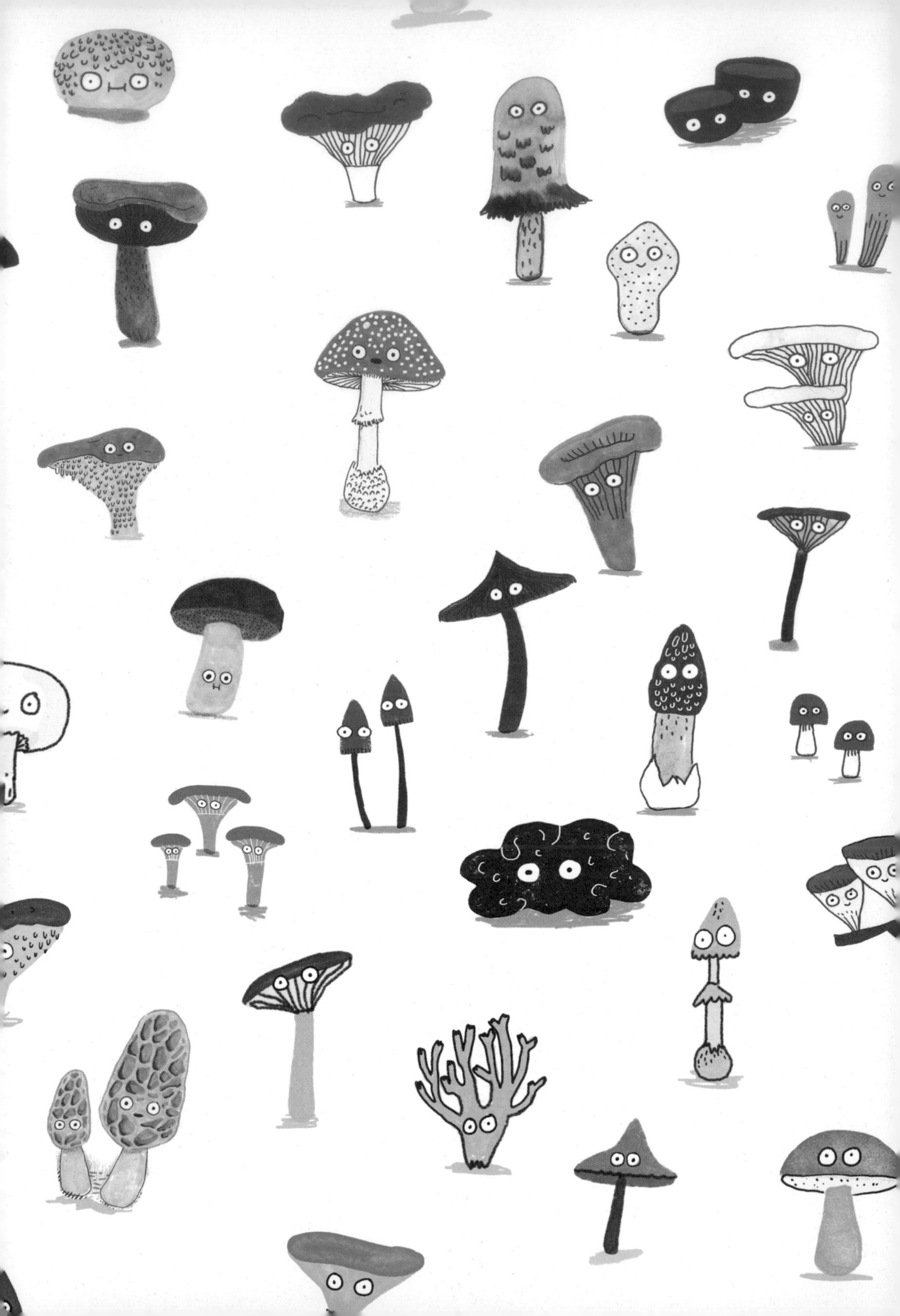